# PINBALL PUNKS

*Dave Anderson*

ISBN: 0692933565
ISBN-13: 9780692933565
Library of Congress Control Number: 2017951788
East Falling, Philadelphia, PA

# NEONICOTINOIDS (THE NEO-NICS)

*Hunger and thirst. That empty, vacant feeling. Earth without its moon. You can ignore it. Suppress it. But it's only a matter of time until it feels like you're internally juggling rusty stilettos, causing everything around you to come to a screeching halt because the only thing that matters is getting what you need to expunge that feeling.*

"Mr. President, the economy seems to be stuck in the doldrums lately. What are you doing to remedy this?"

The president adjusted his tie, took a deep breath, and said, "First of all, I don't know what that word means, and second of all, how many times must I say this? Please, please, please call me Mr. Awesome. Next question."

The next interviewer looked dumbfounded. "Mr...um... Awesome, every facet of society has deteriorated since your inauguration. What are your plans to fix this?"

"You think you can do any better? Huh, do you? Come on, give me some suggestions! That's what I thought. Nothing. This is not easy stuff."

Then out of nowhere, he blurted out with venomous anger, "I will give anybody one hundred thousand dollars who can inspire fresh, new, innovative ideas that work—because apparently, my ideas suck. E-mail me at 1600whitehouse@gov.com."

Mr. Awesome wanted to give the crowd the finger and then throw something at them, but he knew he had already crossed the line with the $100,000. If he added anything else outrageous, the media would begin questioning his mental state. He tried to think of something different, something pleasant to calm himself down. For some strange reason, he thought about neonicotinoids. He had been watching the Science Channel the night before, and they had a special about neonicotinoids and how this insecticide was causing bee colonies to collapse. He felt they were kindred spirits, as he saw his colony collapsing soon if he didn't come up with a solution to save this sinking ship.

# JOHNNY'S NOT HOME

A s Mikey Piss Rat, the bassist for the Piss Rats, walked down the stairs into his dingy basement, a rat scurried across the cold, cracked concrete. It paused and locked eyes with Mikey, and then it disappeared. Mikey had seen cockroaches before but never a rat. When had he vacuumed or swept last?

Procrastinating, he turned on a light and began to play his vintage *Twilight Zone* pinball machine before he cleaned. He loved the sights and sounds as well as the goal of trying to control the chaos that lay within the machine. He imagined the ball was the head of the president and other politicians, and the flippers were fists smashing their heads into the nuts and bolts of the timeless classic game.

The guitarist for the Piss Rats showed up twenty minutes later. Eddie was a punk who thrived on toxic cocktails and telling jokes. He dressed in the standard shock-and-awe punk attire and sported a red Mohawk. Like him, the Mohawk tried hard to stand up but usually was in the process of falling down. His ripped Tragedy band shirt showed off his endless tattoos, while his skintight jeans with holes around the knees were a *fuck you* to the country club people. The final act of defiance was his scuffed black Doc Martens.

*Has there ever been a comedian who was a punk rocker? His jokes are rudimentary, but he could represent the punks in a field they have never ventured into.*

The drummer for the Piss Rats walked down the stairs next. Wally was the die-hard DIY punk. He viewed the world as a place where you live and make the planet better with your actions, or you live and make it worse with your actions. It was that simple. He chose the former. So, did eating animals make the world better? Wally would say no because of factory farms. Did working for a company that endorsed slave labor as part of its business model make the world better? Wally would say no.

Practice had morphed into a search-and-rescue mission for their singer Johnny Piss Rat. He had not been seen or heard from in the past week. The Piss Rats were not terribly concerned because punks were notorious for leaving town. A punk might decide on a whim to get away from it all and hop a freight train, take a Greyhound bus, or drive a car until his or her soul felt worthier. What pestered the Piss Rats was the fact that Johnny was not answering his phone.

They haphazardly went through the motions of their songs minus the vocals. Then, like a defeated army, they marched slowly outside to the city streets in search of their missing band member.

# WEST RIVER DRIVE IS WHERE I COMMIT MY MENTAL CRIMES

Mikey Piss Rat had heard about the president's unorthodox proposition earlier in the day. Hell, how couldn't he or anybody else? The media was bursting at the seams on the verge of an explosion about it. His brain cells went apeshit every time he thought about the vast amount of cash. He could start a business, invest some of it, or just blow it all on endless tours around the globe. He didn't really care about being poor, but he knew if he had some cash, then he would be more optimistic about life and would be able to do things he'd only dreamed about. He thought about 1600whitehouse@gov.com and what exactly he could e-mail them. But then quickly erased the thought. There's no way the president would read his letter, like his idea, decide to meet with him, and then give him all that money. He sat in his beat-up lime-green chair, circa 1950s, that his grandparents had given him and worked on a new song. After twenty minutes, he put his bass down and thought, *With no singer, this is just a waste of time.* He glanced at his watch, and although it was only 9:00 p.m., his motivation was gone for the day. He brushed his teeth and lay in bed reading a *Cometbus*.

Mikey woke up the next morning, and the thought of another long day with nothing to do felt overwhelming. He brewed a strong cup of coffee for motivation and began wandering the city streets. He had read that walking gave Nietzsche and Thoreau new ideas. It was something about the left, right, left, right of his feet. It activated the left and right sides of his brain equally, producing an optimal brain. The sun was out, and he felt rested. Thoughts started circulating inside his brain—how he would pay rent this month with no gigs, Johnny Piss Rat, how he wouldn't mind a girlfriend—and then all of a sudden, like a lightning strike, he thought about e-mailing the president about an idea that had just grown strong and tall inside him.

The idea was simple and straightforward. The manufacture of pinball machines. This would create jobs. Then the money it generated would be allocated and spent by the people, not the politicians. Also, like a dentist extracting a tooth, it would remove people from their homes, and they could socialize with one another instead of their gadgets.

The more he thought about it, the faster he walked. He passed the pier without even stopping to stare out into the burly pool of water. He chain-smoked and decided he better go home now and write the e-mail before his inspiration vanished.

Dear Mr. Awesome,

    My idea at first may appear quite unorthodox and borderline delusional, but let it digest. Society is so divided these days. The people seem lost. They need jobs and need to be social again. They're too glued to their gadgets to hang out with one another. Manufacturing of pinball machines would create jobs and bring people together. The main part of my plan is, each pinball machine represents a part of a town people want to be improved. For example, there are pinball machines for roads, schools, parks, skateboarding, basketball and libraries. Then half the money spent on each machine is allocated toward roads or schools or whatever the people choose, while the other half goes toward paying the employees building the pinball machines. My father was responsible for bringing pinball back from the dead in 1978, so I grew up with the game and know firsthand how great it is. Anyway, I truly believe in my heart this idea can be successful.

Regards, Mike.

Fifteen hours later, his phone giggled and whistled as a text from an unknown number had landed.

Hey Mike,

This is Mr. Awesome, and I just finished reading your idea, and well, I have no clue what to think, really. People like pinball so much it will spur growth in the economy? Honestly, it does sound borderline delusional like you had mentioned. But I am desperate, Mikey. So I would like to hear more about your idea immediately. I know this is probably the greatest moment of your life—i.e., meeting me—so please don't be too nervous. I won't issue a felony if I reject your pinball pitch. I will probably just have the IRS audit you for eternity. Anyway, I would like to meet you tonight at 9:00 p.m., as time is of the essence, Mikey.

# CAREER SUICIDE

Mikey's heart raced as sweat enveloped and engulfed the palms of his hands, as he was positive he was hallucinating. His brain, so desperate for a touch of nostalgia from in his favorite teenage game, must have invented this message. Or did Eddie hide some LSD, and he accidentally ingested it? He went to the bathroom, where he splashed cold water on his face. Immediately feeling more awake and alive, he walked downstairs and picked up his phone again, confident there was no message from the president. But there it remained. He knew he wasn't hired yet. But to just make it this far. It was a miracle.

He texted his bandmates and told them to get over to his place immediately. Being in a band was like a relationship minus the sex, divorce, debt, mortgage, and kids. He didn't want to make any monumental decisions without their opinions and hopefully their approval. He told them to bring a six-pack of beer. He wasn't sure if the president drank, but he knew that he and his bandmates would need it to calm their jangled nerves. Then he texted them again and said, *Just grab a bunch of decent beer.*

*Fancy-pants craft beer to impress the enemy. Pathetic. Real punks drink cheap beer.*

His front door swung open, violently crashing into his wall, as Eddie steamrolled in, spitting a slew of questions. "Are you guaranteed the one hundred thousand dollars? When's he gonna be here? Are you quitting the band? What exactly did you e-mail him that was so revolutionary?"

"Dude, calm down. I don't know much info yet. I would never quit the band, and the idea was manufacturing pinball. You got the beer, right?"

"Pinball?"

Eddie's excitement recoiled and retrieved inward. *Why would the president be so excited over pinball? Did I miss a telegram about pinball being a savior to society?*

"Yeah, dude, I got the beer; we cool."

Wally knocked on the door, and Eddie yelled, "You don't have to knock on the door. Obviously, we're here, and we know it's you." He then gave Mikey a look of *what a jackass.*

Wally took a deep breath to prevent an ulcer from wrapping its oily, gooey tentacles around his intestines. Just when he sat down and began to say something, there was a sharp sound. Like embers floating in the air during a campfire, dust from the side wall next to the door was let loose, producing a slight, quick, transparent evening fog.

It was the doorbell, and the hearts of all three punks began to beat briskly. Mikey put his paws on the doorknob, squeezed, and pulled, showcasing two unknown humans and the president. They all introduced themselves and then opened up some beers. The huge bulky one was the security guard, while the woman was the president's assistant.

Mr. Awesome apologized for his helicopter landing on a few cars in the parking lot and then was in awe of Mikey's decor.

Shimmering orange walls reminded him of Jack-o'-lanterns and the glorious colors that fall produces. The uncomfortable Victorian-style couch was obviously more about aesthetics than comfort. He wondered if Lurch and Uncle Fester would appear next. As retro as it was, there was a modern twist to it with how electric the colors were. Nothing dull. Vivid and radiant. When he was done taking sufficiently large gulps of the eccentric new environment, he asked Mikey to explain his idea further.

Mikey tried to compose himself, but his body felt like it had plugged into a high-voltage amp.

"Every city has endless abandoned warehouses. They're eye-sores and depressing. They don't inspire society. They just remind people of the high unemployment rate from giving China all our jobs. So my plan is transforming them into pinball manufacturing plants. Then charging fifty cents or one dollar a game. Now, this is the unique, awesome part of my idea. Half of that gets allocated toward roads, schools, and the arts, and then half toward paying the pinball employees. So that's a big part of this plan. Each town or city having control over where their money goes. Or rather, the people having the control, not the politicians."

Mike further developed his thought. "Also, this idea will motivate people to be social again. People are so isolated from one another. You can live next to your neighbors for years and never know their names. That's such bullshit. We never hang out with one another. Instead, we'd rather play on our gadgets or watch TV. So my idea will generate jobs, give the people a choice on what aspect of their society needs regeneration and an upswing, and supply them with the materials to be social. I know pinball doesn't sound like a social game, but once you get into playing it, you will compete against others for the highest score while discussing which pinball machines you like the best and other pinball-related stuff. Also, like I said, my dad was responsible for bringing pinball back from the dead, so I have firsthand experience on how superb a game pinball can be."

"Interesting, very interesting. I like it. I really do. It's so outside the box. So, gentlemen, I want all three of you to join me on a two-month tour promoting Mikey's idea. I will pay you each one hundred thousand dollars. But this will not be easy. I expect you to do everything I say. Sign this now."

"Wow, this is so crazy—can we review it first?" asked Mikey.

"Of course, guys," said Mr. Awesome after a long gulp of his Tired Hands brew. "Go into the other room and discuss."

The Piss Rats went into the kitchen with their beers and looked at one another in bewilderment.

"What the fuck! I mean, the money's great, but being the president's slave—I am pretty sure our punk career is over," screamed Eddie.

"Fuck that shit. Who cares? Let's do it. We can take the money and open a killer DIY venue and put it back into punk," Wally responded enthusiastically.

"So Mr. DIY hard-core punk abandons all his ethics at the sight of cash. I always knew you were a fucking sellout, Wally. Hey, Mr. Awesome, come over and kneel down next to Wally's face so I can alternate pissing on each of you since you're obviously both schmucks."

"Shouldn't you be on your twelfth beer by now, you fucking debauchery junkie! Did you not listen to me, Eddie? I said we should take the money and then put it back into punk, you simpleton!"

Eddie felt anger boil like a kettle on a stove. He pushed Wally in the chest, and the two began slamming into the kitchen walls. When a glass fell to the ground and broke, Mr. Awesome's mammoth security guard entered, and the two punks stopped fighting, fearing he would rip them to shreds of pulled pork; their new home would be decaying bone and tendons inside him.

"Everything OK in here?" the security guard asked cautiously.

The brazened Eddie said, "Go eat some 'roids. We didn't request a Neanderthal, so go back to the cave you wandered out of."

The security guard laughed and quickly thought about his days of being a bouncer and how he would purposely rough up loud-mouth punks like the one before him. He calmly walked over to Eddie, who immediately apologized. The guard wanted to punch him in the stomach and knock the wind out of him, but he couldn't afford to lose another job because of rogue violence. He stomped out of the kitchen, and the punks were alone again to make the biggest decision of their lives.

"OK, everyone just calm down," said a frazzled Mikey. Let's just read the contract."

As they read it, they realized that the gist of it was that the Piss Rats would listen and do whatever Mr. Awesome said.

Mikey looked at his bandmates, who didn't say anything, still soaking in anger, so he grabbed a pen and added, "As long as it doesn't involve murder, rape, theft, or anything else against the law."

"What about Johnny, though?" questioned Eddie. "If we commit to this and Johnny shows up, then he's going to be super pissed at us."

"I love Johnny as much as anybody else," said Wally. "But him not answering his phone and Mr. Awesome demanding an answer ASAP leaves us in a real tough dilemma."

Reflection on the current situation caused internal turbulence. Abandoning the search for Johnny. Gridlock on playing shows and recording new tunes. Joining forces with what they loathed.

The Piss Rats looked at one another and then looked around the kitchen. Mikey visually inspected his blender and wondered when the last time he had cleaned it. Eddie studied the micro-wave and wondered if there were any frozen burritos in the freezer. Wally gazed at the kitchen walls and noticed all the little bursts of food splattered all over, and he wondered when the last time anyone scrubbed the walls.

They were shaken from their requiem when Eddie let loose a smelly fart.

"What the fuck, Eddie!" yelled Mikey.

Wally followed with "You fuckin' asshole—listen, are we doing this or what? I can't take this smell any longer."

"Sure, whatever, let's just sell our souls for the almighty dollar, fuckin' traitors," Eddie said, feeling defeated.

They walked out of the kitchen, and Eddie quietly muttered, "I guess nobody cares that I have a wife, huh?"

"Here you go, Mr. Awesome. Just added a line," said Mikey.

"Yes, of course, no breaking the law. Well, I must say, Piss Rats, this is very exciting. Are you guys excited?" Before they could answer, Mr. Awesome said, "Of course you are. You get to hang out with the president all day and night for the next two months. Here is a little advance money, since I assume you're probably broke. I will pick you up at ten a.m. tomorrow."

Eddie bit his tongue and fought the urge to tell Mr. Awesome that the Piss Rats didn't need him and his money and all the corrupt bullshit that came along with it. *We rather be broke and on the streets than comply with your sick war games.* But a little part of him felt relief. It wasn't easy being married and being a broke punk. Clash was supportive of his lifestyle, but a little part of him felt like a lousy failed husband every time he told her that they couldn't afford to go on vacation or couldn't buy something for the house because the money just wasn't there.

Everybody left leaving Mikey alone in his house with his thoughts ricocheting off every angle and corner of his skull. He retrieved a pad of paper and wrote down everything that had transpired in case things went awry and the law was involved. He wanted a judge and jury to know that he went into this scenario with no ill thoughts of crime and thievery. He walked to his desk, pulling out an envelope and slapping a stamp on it. It was addressed to his brother.

He texted him and said, "Hey, when you get this envelope, do not open it. Just keep it safe; it's very important. I will explain it later over some beers. Thanks."

# SHAKEDOWN

The next morning the tour bus arrived. It was a large gray bus. All gray. Mikey was hoping the bus might have some badass pinball machine painted on the side. Something to tell the world things were changing. Changing for the better. The people were pissed and were doing what the politicians should have been doing all along. Coming up with ideas to enhance and revise society. But it was just a long, big gray bus.

Mikey had four bags filled to the brim with clothes, books, and shoes. Like all punks, his gear was covered with stickers and patches with his favorite bands. Smoke or Fire. Aus-Rotten. The Pist. The Weakerthans. Hot Water Music. Blanks 77. The Generators. The Showcase Showdown. Amebix. A Wilhelm Scream. No Use For a Name. Boy Sets Fire. Jawbreaker. Antisect. Sick of it All. Leftover Crack. Pears. Nausea. Flatfoot 56. Nightfall. Zex. Barry Bliss. Vision. Zero Boys. Authority Zero. At the Drive-In. Bear vs. Shark. Blitz. Leatherface. Blood Pressure. EEL. After the Fall. Stiff Little Fingers. Good Riddance. Ramones. World Inferno/Friendship Society. H2O. J Church. Modern Life Is War. Bishops Green. The

Briggs. We Must Dismantle All This! Streetlight Manifesto. Anti Cimex. Satanic Surfers.

Mr. Awesome walked out of the bus, shook hands with Mikey, and told him to make himself comfortable. Mikey walked inside, dropped his bags on the floor, and took a seat in what he assumed was the main living room. He looked at his new surroundings. No dirt or stains or trash or empty beer cans like the Piss Rats' tour bus. He got up and walked down the hall and saw a legit bar along with a kitchen. The twenty tons of metal began to move oil through the engine, and the rubber and gears propelled it forward as Mikey stared out the window, wondering if he would ever return home.

They picked up Eddie and Wally next. Mr. Awesome took a seat opposite them. Nobody said anything. Both sides eyeing the other. Looking for weakness. Napalm and flamethrowers within arm's reach. But they were on the same team now. They needed to get along.

"So I sense some tension between us," Mr. Awesome said.

"Yeah, 'cause punks hate politicians; it's in our DNA to clash with you," said Eddie.

"Well, how about you do some of your comedy act. Rumor is you're pretty good."

"Nah, brah, only when I am wasted will I do that shit."

"Well then, let's begin the drinking." Mr. Awesome motioned for them to follow him to another section of the bus that was about as close to a real bar as it came.

"Piss Rats, this is all yours, my friends. Drink all you want when you want. But if you screw up on the job, the booze is gone."

Eddie looked at the bar, and it was like sun replacing clouds.

*Two days without substance. Need food soon. But what food has become, I'd almost rather starve. Soon I will do it.*

"Isn't it a little early to start drinking? It's like, what, twelve thirty," protested Wally.

"Wally, it's called day drinking. Ever heard of it? Jeez," retorted Eddie.

"Guys, relax. Wally, you don't have to start drinking; nobody has to drink. It was just a suggestion," said Mr. Awesome.

"Day drinking, day drinking, day drinking," chanted Eddie. His Achilles' heel had now been compromised, and he would stop at nothing until it was fully compromised.

They all cracked open a beer and tried to settle into their new routine. There was silence for the first few minutes until the gears became lubricated as their blood began to turn black from the dark beers they were sipping on. Some small chatter finally erupted.

"So how is the band going? Can I hear a song?" asked Mr. Awesome.

"Does anybody have "Shakedown" on their iPod?" asked Eddie.

"I have it," said Mikey.

Yeah they come
Yeah they go
They speak words
But words don't flow
They creak and they crack
Rusty Nails and Rusty Tacks
Rusty Nails and Rusty Tacks
Rusty Nails and Rusty Tacks
Will be hammered in our backs
As the Law says don't react
'Cause they're above and you're below
That's the way it goes
They're above and you're below

That's the way it goes
*How High How High*
*Ooooh How High will they Climb?*
*Shakedown all the Leaves*
*Leave Nothing for You or Me*
Woah Woah Woah Woah Woah Woah
These thoughts they circle round
Like hawks they dive on down
Attacking me every day leaving me in dismay
That what I see is what I see
And what I hear is what I hear
What I see Is what I see
And what I hear Is what I hear
*How High How High*
*Ooooh How High will they Climb?*
*Shakedown all the Leaves*
*Leave Nothing for You or Me*
Woah Woah Woah Woah Woah Woah
Face-to-Face
I see a face, but no one's home
A knock on the door but that door stays closed
*How High How High*
*Ooooh How High will they Climb?*
*Shakedown all the Leaves*
*Leave Nothing for You or Me*
Woah Woah Woah Woah Woah Woah
Under a streetlight
In the morning sun bright
There's always a handshake and a grin
Steady diet looking thin
Let's Turn Away Let's Turn Away
Every minute, every hour, every day
Let's Turn Away Let's Turn Away

Every minute, every hour, every day
Let's Turn Away Let's Turn Away
And we can find a better way yeah yeah yeah yeah

The president had a sinister grin on his face.

"Well, boys, certainly not my style of music, but it sounds like you worked hard on it. And the lyrics—I suppose they're punches and jabs at my crew down in DC? Fair enough." He gripped the bottle so tight that it seemed about ready to shoot shrapnel in every direction.

Everybody cracked open another beer to alleviate the tension that was still loitering and panhandling.

"Anyway, it's just a song; there are millions of these types of songs. Can you explain some more about this tour?" asked Wally in an attempt to let a dove fly out and bring some peace.

"Well, Piss Rats, we're really not going to change much of what Mikey's vision is. So we're going to take some of the abandoned buildings in cities around America and begin manufacturing pinball machines. This will improve the economy by providing jobs. Then those machines will be put in strategic locations around America. Fifty cents a game. Half the money will be put back into the community, and half will pay the employees building the pinball machines. We then hope to have them put in bars, grocery stores, college campuses, and any other areas that are interested. So if you're upset about your community having shitty roads and crime and bad schools, come play pinball, and your money will be allocated toward fixing these things."

*It's actually not a bad idea. Well done, Mikey. I feel like these are the kinds of things our "leaders" should be coming up with.*

"But where does the money come from to start all of this? You already spent three hundred thousand dollars on us, and it's going to cost a ton to implement this plan," said Wally whose peace dove was now plummeting from the sky with broken wings.

"Well, there is, um, see, boys, for important stuff like this, there are certain monies hidden away that are to be used for things of this nature, so I am just borrowing from that fund," said Mr. Awesome.

"He's probably just printing more money or plundering our tax money—more of the same. This idea and every idea by every politician is pure horseshit," said an angry Wally as he walked to the back of the bus.

*It felt like rain on a hot summer day. His dormant dying cells bounced into action to retrieve his new food source.*

Wally flushed the toilet, and as he was walking away, he thought he saw a rat hanging around the porcelain. Used to rodents, bugs, and dirt, he just ignored it. When he returned, a series of shots were poured.

"Wally and Eddie, I know you're frustrated with society, but I am trying, and I just need your help these next two months because I think this idea has potential. Also, remember, this was all Mikey's idea too. He e-mailed this to me, so yeah."

"But you're the president! I am sure people offer up stupid ideas like this daily," protested Wally.

"What the fuck, Wally. This is a good idea," said Mikey.

"It is, Mikey. I apologize. It's just, where is the money going to come from to start all this up?"

Mikey chugged his beer and muttered, "No fuckin' clue." He then grabbed a shot before everybody else and nodded to the president.

"Thank you, Mikey," said Mr. Awesome.

*Punks getting drunk with the president for the next two months. When Maximum Rock and Roll finds out about this, the Piss Rats will be vagabonds and vagrants.*

Everybody was now sufficiently wasted. Eddie was spiraling and swiveling to one of his favorite bands, Mischief Brew. Their brand of medieval gypsy punk acted like a pungi and Eddie, the cobra.

Mikey's mind wandered to the cute female who was the president's assistant named Ava. She wore green Converse shoes, a white tank top, and black jeans so tight it looked like her legs were painted black. A small tattoo peeked out from under the bottom of her jeans near the top of her shoes. Could she have some counterculture vibes in her? He quickly launched that thought into a dingy desolate part of his brain where things go to die. She was the president's assistant; no way could she be anything but another sheep. Another person he would have nothing in common with.

Around 7:00 p.m., Mr. Awesome walked away and returned a minute later with some weed. "Anybody wanna kick this party up a notch?"

"No fuckin' way. The president smokes?" Eddie said with a laugh.

"Why do you think nothing gets done in DC? We're high all the time! Just kidding, of course. As you've heard, weed is basically legal everywhere now, so this is not a crime, really. Plus, it helps me loosen up and live for the moment instead of constantly forecasting my next move."

He lit the blunt and passed it around. Everybody smoked it down to the nub. A haze pasted itself on their brains. They listened to the music without much movement.

Eddie's nervous energy began to kick in, and he pestered Mr. Awesome about doing something cool. Mr. Awesome, in turn, told Eddie there was a dart board if anybody was interested. They all agreed that darts would be a boisterous jolly time.

A drunken Eddie asked Mr. Awesome if he always wanted to be president.

Mr. Awesome's brain went to kidnap some words, but instead, it just drifted out to orbit.

As a child, he never dreamed of being the president. His passion was trash. His OCD was so intense, he had to clean and organize everything. His brain's main focus, though, was trash. If he saw it on the streets or in a park—anywhere—he immediately had to clean it up. He would run into traffic if there was a feral cigarette butt and wander his neighborhood daily, picking up any trash he saw lingering around. At first, his parents ignored his "hobby," but at age fourteen, when he started talking regularly to the trashman who picked up his parents' trash and asking for advice about what trash cans were primo, they began to show some concern.

"Don't you want to play video games or hang out with people your own age?" they would ask him.

"Mom, there's just so much trash in the world and so little time to clean it up. I just don't have time for anything else."

So his parents would hit the streets before him, hoping that if there was no trash around, he would have to act like a normal teenager. With no trash in his neighborhood, he would stay after school and help the janitors out.

In college, he finally was able to get a part-time job on campus, cleaning up the various trash cans. He would check on them every few hours. He became known around campus as the weird trash-man student who seemed to enjoy picking up trash. A frat asked him to pledge, but he told them he just didn't have time; there was so much trash to pick up. So they showed him their frat. Seeing all that trash caused an itch that would need to be scratched. Endless beer bottles and trash overflowing out of every trash can. He joined the following month, and anytime somebody gave him a tough time about his strange hobby, his frat brothers would stick up for him and crack any skulls who messed with their frat brother, for they loved having him around. They never had to clean a single thing. Their grades even improved because they were able to focus now on just two things: partying and going to class.

After law school, he took a few weeks off to think about his future, but all he could think about was trash. His first job was on the city council, where he didn't really care about anything but trash and how his part of the city looked. While his fellow city council members were working on education, budgets, and crime, he would be going out in the city, picking up trash, cleaning up parks, and doing other general maintenance. The people would see him out every day picking up trash, and they thought, *Finally, somebody in office cares about their community and job.*

He quickly rose up in government, and when everyone around pushed him to run for president, he figured he could then clean up all the trash on earth. But people were not trash. As president, he could not walk around the DC streets picking up trash. He had to deal with real-world problems, which were humans, not trash. When society had critical issues, he couldn't just walk out of his house with an empty trash bag; he had to come up with solutions.

"Well, Eddie, I wanted to be president to clean up and fix the world."

"Wow, that's the most boring thing I have ever heard." Eddie grabbed his beer, took a long swig, and said, "How about this, Mr. Awesome: What's the craziest shit you ever did in the White House?"

"Eddie, come on, man; leave him alone," said Wally.

"Thanks, Wally, but this is a fun question. Give me a minute to ponder, and I also want the craziest thing you ever did on tour," said Mr. Awesome.

"Oh, I know already," said Eddie. "After this one gig, before I was married, I was drinking at the bar when this group of punks came up to me and started calling me a poser punk. They said real punks live in squats. I told them real punks did this. I went up to everyone in the bar, grabbed what they were drinking, and chugged it. I drank at least thirty people's drinks in ten minutes. The entire bar wanted to kick my ass. Then I vomited all over these punks and told them it sucked that their squat didn't have a washing machine 'cause being covered in puke was pretty fuckin' nasty."

"What the hell! Holy shit—that's so fucked up," said Mr. Awesome, who was swimming in a pool of laughter. "Well, first, you can never repeat this. So, there's a one-lane bowling alley in the White House, and me and the wife play every week. Well, this one time, I collected items from other presidents around the White House and then put them on the bowling balls without telling my wife about it. So she thinks it's just another weekly bowling game, and then there are all these bowling balls with different objects on them. So, for Lincoln, I was like, "I was responsible for the Emancipation Proclamation and turning three million slaves into free people, and now my top hat is on a big heavy ball? Oh no, you're going to roll this ball now with my hat on it?"

"So for George Washington, lemme guess. You put his wig on a bowling ball?"

"Actually, Eddie, even though wigs were fashionable in the 1700s, he never wore one. He actually powered his hair white because it was red."

"The first president was a ginger?"

"Yup, Washington was a ginger, Eddie. And that ginger drafted the Constitution, started the American Revolution, was a soldier and commander-in-chief, and is considered one of the founding fathers of the United States."

"Now, Eddie, John Adams wore a wig."

"Who the hell is John Adams? Was he my seventh-grade math teacher?"

"Ha-ha. Fair question, Edward. He was the not very popular, as you just showed us, first vice president and second president. A poor dresser as well I might add. Anyway, I took Adams's wig, put in on a bowling bowl, and then threw the ball down the lane, saying, "I am a Harvard graduate and scholar of law. I demand dignity!""

"That's rad shit, man. So presidents do have some wittiness tucked away for a rainy day. That's encouraging, no doubt."

"Correct, Eddie, we are normal humans."

At 9:00 p.m. they all decided to call it a day.

"See, Wally, when you day drink, you then also usually crash early," mumbled a sloshed Eddie as he floundered and wobbled his way back to his new home.

# ALCHEMY

Mikey woke up to use the bathroom around 7:00 a.m. As he got out of his bed, he felt a craving for liquids so intense he didn't notice white bandages on his fingers until he lifted the glass of water to his lips. He could still move them and function fine, but what the hell happened to his fingers last night? He hastily used the bathroom, as he was edgy and shaky mentally from the previous night's debauchery and was dying to know how his bandmates' hands were doing. He scrambled from the bathroom to see the other Piss Rats suffering the same affliction. Frantically he woke them. "Guys, our fingers, they're bandaged up. Does anybody remember anything about how this happened?"

They shook their heads gingerly.

Mikey ran away from them to find Mr. Awesome. He saw the president's assistant first. She had a tank top on and short jean shorts. He tried to not focus on her amazing body.

Out of breath from his short run, he stopped a foot from her, waving his hand like he was trying to signal a cab. "What is this! What the fuck is going on here?"

"Oh, you're fine, Mikey; just a simple procedure, no worries. Mr. Awesome will explain it when he gets up. He's very hungover right now, so let's keep the volume down."

Mikey felt a bit relieved but was still in a panic state. After just one night, his bandmates were being experimented on like it was the fifties, and they were mental patients.

"What did he say?" asked Eddie.

"Apparently, the president is still sleeping and very hungover, but Ava insists it was just a simple procedure, and there is nothing to worry about."

They all decided to go back to their beds and lie down. Like the president, they were frail, fragmented fugitives, too frail to abandon their headaches and hangovers and replace them with fresh, fertile brains.

A few hours later, Mr. Awesome strolled back to their side of the bus in a pair of boxers with no shirt on. "Piss Rats, you crazy bastards," he said, laughing. "What a night, wow! Let's get some breakfast and shake off this hangover."

"What the fuck did you do to our hands, Mr. Asshole!" shouted Wally.

"Oh yeah, you're fine; you can remove the bandages," said Mr. Awesome as he strolled away.

"What happened!" yelled Mikey.

Forced to stop walking, he turned back to face the bunch of spooked punks and said, "Mike, you're at about a ten right now. Can you lower it to a four?" Mr. Awesome rubbed his forehead as if his hands could magically remove the pounding inside his skull.

"I had you guys injected with a highly potent metal so your hands can play pinball for hours—shit, days—and never become tired. This is extremely safe. People in all industries use it. The army uses it so they can practice shooting and never become tired. Most athletes get it around their knees, and most importantly, porn stars…well, let's just say there is a reason why they're so large and in charge."

"Really?" said Eddie. "If we're successful with this pinball bullshit, can I get my cock injected with it? I wanna be a porn star!" Eddie tried gyrating his hips and moving his lips, daydreaming about being the biggest porn star ever.

"Eddie, what the fuck, man. Come on, this is serious. The president did this without our approval," said Wally.

"Enough about this trivial procedure. It's time we prepare for our first big meeting—rally—whatever you want to call it—in Detroit in three days. So banish the mental cobwebs from last night, and be ready in an hour to play pinball all day."

The president and Ava walked away with conviction.

# INDIANS LOST PRESIDENT'S SLAVE IS THE COST

The bus chugged and chugged down the highway and then rolled into the parking lot of what looked at first glance to be a standard strip mall with the traditional stores consisting of pizza, Chinese, subs, and yoga. However, upon further investigation, there was one store that was out of step with the rest. This store called itself Pinball Gallery. Mr. Awesome explained that they would be practicing the next few days there, for he had rented out the entire establishment.

They entered the albino store, and before they could remove their leather and denim jackets, Mikey was already bullying a pinball machine with demonic fever.

"Watch and learn, suckas," said Mikey, feeling confident and commanding, like the leader of a ragtag group of mischief marauders.

Wally and Eddie watched Mikey play for a few minutes before the bright colors and shiny metals from all the different machines attracted their immediate attention.

As they walked around slowly, looking at all the machines, they couldn't help but feel transported back in time, looking at the themes on the pinball machines. *Addams Family. Attack from Mars. Batman. Wizard of Oz. Ghostbusters. Funhouse. Indiana Jones. Creature from the Black Lagoon.*

After an hour, none of their hands were tired. Maybe it was a smart idea for Mr. Awesome to inject their hands with metal or whatever the hell it was.

"OK, Piss Rats, take a ten-minute break. Mikey, since you're obviously the talented pinball player, I want you to teach the other two for the rest of the day."

The Piss Rats spent their ten minutes using the bathroom and discussing their new environment. Usually, there would be a chorus of chatter about new song ideas, gigs, and politics, but now they discussed Mr. Awesome and their current predicament. They were nervous about what they would wake up to tomorrow if after just one night they were already being experimented on.

Wally looked at his cell phone. The stopwatch had reached ten minutes, and he said they should get back to practicing. Eddie wanted to rip into Wally about how lame a punk he was for setting his cell-phone stopwatch but thought better of it. He really should be nicer to Wally; he loved him like a brother and knew Wally's heart was made of gold, but he just wished Wally was a little more reckless and carefree. He also knew that with age, people change and become more responsible. Eddie quickly lit up one more smoke, ignoring Wally's demand. He might not protest Wally verbally, but silently he would most definitely do it.

"Look at the display," said Mikey. "If we're playing on games from the nineties onward, the display will give you hints on what to do next.

"Listen to the sounds. Machines from the late seventies onward were electronically designed to produce sounds. So start to make mental connections on when you hit something, the sound it makes, and the points you get.

"Learn the rules. Ava, can you print out the modern rules of pinball, please?"

Ava looked at Mr. Awesome, not knowing if she was now the assistant to the Piss Rats as well as the president. Mr. Awesome gave her a nod of approval.

"Sure," she said.

"Master the basics of flipping. Don't flip both flippers. Only flip the flipper that can make contact with the ball. Then let the flipper down. Holding it up leaves open an area for the ball to slide under.

"Practice catching the ball. This can take time to learn, but with our metal fingers, you can master this quickly. So as the ball is pummeling chaotically at you, hold the flipper out and try to catch it. This will give you time to plan your next move, take a sip from a beverage, adjust your hat or smoke a cig.

Eddie's brain became blasé listening to Mikey's attempt at teaching them pinball. He hated when others tried teaching him anything. *Just let me figure it out myself, trial and error.* He started thinking of new jokes.

"So here is how you know disgustingly rich business men, celebrities, sport stars and politicians hate you. They haven't pooled their millions and trillions together to invent bulletproof clothing. In Chicago, there is a person shot every few minutes. If these people, really gave a shit about you, there would be bulletproof jackets, shorts, shoes, sunglasses, gold teeth, chains, hats and jeans. Then open up boxing rings in each neighborhood with signs that read, *Real men fight with their fists, not guns.* And actually, I would add a glow in the dark sword to the mix. Imagine walking down an alley late at night after some beers and some thugs think they see an easy target. But upon further investigation they see a man with a glow in the dark sword. They would definitely think twice about fucking with a dude holding a sword. If they still were brave enough, well, when a few fingers go flying off, they know it's a real sword so they begin to shot you. But that doesn't work either as the bullets just bounce off you. Honestly, don't tell my wife, she will make fun of me, but late at night, I walk around with a tennis racket for safety. I just hope none of my neighbors are tennis play-ers and see me carrying a racket and ask to play tennis with me someday! He then pictured himself winning the Noble Peace Prize and spending a majority of his speech talking about how much smarter he was then Wally and how he wasn't just a drunk punk like Wally advertised him being.

"You ever wonder: if your GPS was a person or had a soul, would it, like, try to beat the shit out of you or eternally curse you when you turn it off before you reach the final destination as most peo-ple do? Like the GPS works super hard for hours and hours, giving you directions, and then, just when it's time to reach its reward, the end location, people turn it off. It's like running a marathon, see-ing the finish line, and saying, "OK, close enough," and giving up. I have to be honest, when I use the GPS for hours and hours and my wife turns it off just before I reach my destination, I wonder if the GPS is going to give me some kind of bad luck, like a black cat crossing your path or failing to respond to a chain letter. So every time my wife goes to turn it off before we park the car, I do my best to sidetrack her to keep it on and thus avoiding any possible bad luck the GPS tries to dish out.

*Ugh*, he thought, *kinda dumb. Or is it? I guess I will have to test it out. I never know if these jokes are good or not without a live audience.*

"Learn to aim. So after you have learned to catch the ball, if you want to aim the ball to the left, then release the ball and quickly hit it. If you want to aim the ball to the right, then release it and hit it at the tip of the flipper.

"Get aggressive. It's perfectly normal to nudge and tilt the machine. It may sound impossible to move a machine so big, but with the proper amount of pressure, you can save a ball you might otherwise have lost. And if you're too aggressive, there are sensors on the machine that will tell you to calm down.

"Stance. Figure out what stance is best for you. Do you like a barstool nearby to use if your feet and knees get tired? Do you like to hover over the machine, or do you like certain shoes, clothing?"

"When Mr. Awesome hooks up my porn cock," said Eddie, "my stance will be this." Eddie thrust his hips back and forth at the machine. "Hey, Ava, come here so I can show everyone exactly how my 'stance' will be."

Ava picks up a hairbrush and launches it at Eddie. He ducks as it hit the wall, generating a rambunctious clang.

"Everyone calm down and take a break," said Mr. Awesome.

They practiced the rest of the day. Mr. Awesome and Ava watched the entire time to ensure there was no discord in the fluidity.

Around 7:00 p.m., Mr. Awesome told them they could stop for the day.

"Damn," said Wally, "I never thought I would spend an entire day playing pinball. That was pretty damn cool. Thanks, Mr. Awesome."

*Thanking the president of the United States of America for allowing pinball playing all day—where the hell am I? This must be a nightmare.*

"Wally, I am glad you enjoyed it. I was a little worried you guys might think this was dumb and not care.

"Punks don't give up," interjected Eddie. "Actually, never mind. We usually do give up a lot and go get drunk instead—just easier. Speaking of booze, we partying tonight, Awesome, or what?"

"It's Mr. Awesome, and I don't want to party tonight, but I think you guys earned it. Mikey especially."

"Yeah, no problem. I wish I could do this every day. Get paid to just hang out with my band while teaching them about pinball ball. Hell yeah. This was a cool ass day."

*I think I'd rather at this point go get food than listen to this bullshit.*

Next to the Pinball Gallery was the Rats' favorite vegan joint: Su Tao Café. "I can't believe Su Tao is right next to the Pinball Gallery, I always leave this place stuffed to the brim, smiling, and with a grin," said Wally.

After dinner they all met up in the bar area and cracked open some beers. The mood was light and airy, like a slice of freshly baked bread. A drastic change from yesterday's tense mood at the outset.

"So, Mr. Awesome," said Mikey, "we're really curious and a little nervous about this first rally. I mean, we're going to be on TV, I assume?"

"You will be on TV briefly, yes. We need to keep that to the minimum, though, to ensure nobody finds out a punk band is helping me. Down the toilet all our careers would go. It is certainly normal to be nervous, but if we have another successful day of practice tomorrow, I am confident things will be smooth with the pinball part. After that, you will just have to learn some dialogue. See, guys, at each meeting or speech or rally—you know what, I am not sure what it's called, so let's just say at each city—you're going to be dressed up differently to promote pinball. Actually, let's call them rallies. So for the first rally, I want you dressed up as blue-collar workers who just finished a long, honest day's work and want to hang out and play some pinball. Ava will be helping you with your clothing and reviewing your dialogue so it flows nicely. The lines are easy, but remember, there will be tons of eyes and cameras on you; it's important to practice the lines so you're not nervous and rusty. Then, Piss Rats, unfortunately, makeup. Like I said, staying in disguise is mega vital to success. Enough business, though. Let's do some shots!"

The night spun out of control fairly quickly after Eddie brought out his personal stash of blow. Everybody, even Ava, was doing lines and slamming beers. The music seemed to get louder in relation to the beers being crushed. Eddie always had to be the DJ when alcohol was in his system. If he didn't have on catchy punk music he could sing and dance to, he turned into a grouchy, grumpy earth dweller. Tonights playlist consisted of Cock Sparrer, Oxymoron, The Suicide Machines and Antagonizers ATL. Eddie was standing on any furniture that could support him singing his drunken heart out. When the Misfits came on, he was perched on top of the refrigerator like a bat for the beginning of the song and once the chorus came on he leaped off it falling to the floor in maniacal laughter.

Mikey was sneaking looks at Ava, and she noticed it and asked Mikey, "So what exactly are you punks rebelling against? I mean, I don't—I am not trying to be rude or anything—but dressing in black with spikes and Mohawks while being drunk and crude all the time isn't exactly changing the world."

Mikey's head felt like it was filled with honey and a thousand bees were buzzing in and out of it. He had to find a way to not spill the honey and have the thousand bees sting Ava.

"Well, I guess we just don't support a system that makes you work five days and only have off two days. That doesn't mean we're lazy, either. It just means we have hobbies and passions, and when you're working all the time, well, it can be tough to find enough time for doing shit you dig. Why don't we work four days, twelve hours instead of five days, eight hours? This would give everybody one more free day and cut down on cars on the road, thus helping the environment. Everyone claims to care about the environment, yet most people work 5 days a week when they could easily work four days a week instead.

"But you guys do have regular normal jobs that you work five days a week, and I imagine sometimes six days a week, so obviously you're not even following that."

"Wally only does volunteer work for causes he supports, so you're wrong, actually."

*Hell yeah, your wrong!*

"We're just against a boss or CEO exploiting us so he can be richer while paying us just enough to survive."

"Well, if you callous up those hands, you can become the boss," countered Ava.

"Maybe it's in our DNA, but the Piss Rats are just anti most of what society is. I don't know what else to tell ya. We're not lazy or drunks; we just don't like what society has become, and our music and appearance reflect that. Anyway, how did you become the assistant to the president, Ava?"

Ava ground her teeth. She tried digesting the question and thinking about a response. But all she could think and feel was her heart racing from the many poisons skinny-dipping in her blood. She wanted to tell Mikey everything. But she had done blow only a few times before and was afraid she would tell him one long rambling thirty-minute sentence. Then she would become paranoid and pray for a dagger to end the paranoia. So she just said, "Oh, it's a boring story. Maybe I'll tell you later."

"Eddie, how about some of that comedy? You're definitely drunk. I mean, I just saw you singing along to the radio," commented Mr. Awesome.

"Dude, this is not the radio. It's Tim fuckin' Barry! Shit is mega righteous and legit. But yeah, I guess I can tell some jokes to you filthy animals."

They turned the music down, and all eyes were on Eddie. He stumbled around for a minute, and then his lawless and turbulent face produced a sinister grin, dumping out a pile of words for the eager public to chew and swallow.

"So I was at the Olive Garden last night and noticed there were no olive dishes on the menu. What's next? No burgers at Burger King? Welcome to Burger King, the leader in seafood. Welcome to Pizza Hut, we now have vegetarian hot dogs in addition to our vast selection of beef hot dogs. McDonald's, today's special is green curry."

Everybody laughed, even Mikey and Wally, who had heard that joke many times before.

"So I belong to a gym and have been getting annoyed lately at all the people who will wait five minutes with their flashers on to try to get a close parking spot. Like this isn't fucking Ikea. You're not carrying tons of crap to your car. Plus, if you're afraid of walking one hundred feet, perhaps the gym is the wrong place for you.

Speaking of cars, what's up with those concrete blocks people put under cars when parked on hills. So a fifty-pound rock is going to slow down a four thousand pound car?"

"Those rocks are incredibly successful in preventing major catastrophes," shouted Mr. Awesome.

Eddie looked feral and brutish. A beast about to tear apart his prey. He twitched and acted like he swallowed a pool ball. Then he said, "Anyway, that's just a little of my shit, I am going to sleep now."

*Here's a new joke. The Piss Rats' career.*

# EGYPT IS THE REASON

The lazy, hazy sun shone on the bus, puncturing through the blinds. Movement and activity occurred in slow motion. Moans and groans from the previous night's damage were slow to flicker and fade away. Coffee began to flow. Mr. Awesome told the Rats they had an hour before the day's activities would commence.

"So, Rats, tomorrow is the big day! Here's how it will go down. I will be giving a speech at eight p.m. in a Detroit warehouse that has been renovated. Pinball manufacturing has already begun there. So in a sense, it's like a brewery. In one area pinball machines are manufactured, and there's another spot where you can actually play the games and hang out. So you guys will be dressed like normal blue-collar workers, and the media will interview you. Here is a copy of potential questions the media will be given to select from, along with answers."

The Rats reviewed the questions and answers with a dedicated, serious demeanor. They knew it was time to earn all that money and keep their word. Ethics might not be important for politicians, but for punks, it was all they had. So they put on their headphones and studied hard.

"So how's it going, guys?" asked Mr. Awesome.

"Yeah, fine, whatever. We got this shit," said Eddie.

"Excellent—take a break for lunch, and then, Mikey, please start the pinball training again."

They went into the kitchen and began ripping open packages and twisting jars. Water boiled on the stove. The microwave buzzed loudly like cicadas in the summer heat.

"This is probably the best I will ever eat. I mean, the selection is ridiculous. Endless veggie meats and pasta. The freezer is overflowing with berries, and there are half a dozen protein powders for smoothies in the corner. The cupboards are stocked with snacks. Look at how many different kinds of chips there are. There's like a hundred bananas. Clash is going to call me a little chub chub when I see her again."

"A what?" asked Wally.

"You heard me the first time, Wally. I am not repeating myself."

After eating, they began practicing pinball again.

"Wally, try to catch the ball when you're this late in the game. I noticed you were getting a little antsy. By catching the ball, you can pause and regroup."

As Mikey was teaching the other two punks about pinball, Mr. Awesome's brain pulled the plug and disconnected from his device. He thought about the ocean and the waves coming to shore and crashing, producing a soapy, fuzzy, cloudy texture. He picked up a jellyfish and felt its squishy spine. Then he was transported to Egypt, and he was on a camel walking past huge pyramids. All of a sudden, the camel was climbing up the pyramid and then began speaking. "Hey, Mr. Awesome, I hope you enjoy your ride up the pyramids. I don't do this for everybody, you know. It's really hard on my body since I am a camel. Really, I should be riding you up this pyramid."

Eddie noticed Mr. Awesome had checked out, so he began to untie his shoelaces so he could then tie them together so when Mr. Awesome went to walk, he would trip, and Eddie would laugh for days and days.

When Ava noticed this, she slapped Eddie on the side of his head, and Eddie fell into Mr. Awesome.

"Oh hey, guys, sorry, was just thinking about Iraq and Afghanistan and endangered species. It's not easy being president."

They went out to a Mediterranean restaurant for dinner. Mr. Awesome had a fake moustache and hat on so nobody would notice him. He hated when he had to dress up because he craved vociferous slabs of attention. Everyone was burned out from the past few nights of partying, so the mood was distant and adrift. A lonely one-manned ship with no waves. The Piss Rats all ordered falafel meals, while the president ordered lamb, and Ava ordered a chicken plate.

After dinner, they went back and relaxed with some TV and reading. Mikey and Ava sat on the couch, watching some random movie while playing with their phones. Wally lay in bed reading, while Eddie messed with his laptop. Mr. Awesome took a stroll through the bus, making some small talk and observations, and he ended up at Eddie's room. He decided to ask Eddie what he was doing, knowing the punk was probably up to something mischievous and ghoulish.

"Oh, you don't want to know, Mr. Awesome. It's not exactly intelligent shit like you're accustomed to."

Like a kid begging his parents, Mr. Awesome said, "Come on—just show me."

"Fine, but I warned you. Whenever I have a hangover or feel like messing with the drones called humans, I like to write fucked-up reviews on Amazon and see if they get published. Usually, I get an e-mail from them about how my review was inappropriate, and then I get a warning, or they ban me. Then

I have to register a new account under a new e-mail. I did these tonight."

"For a pellet gun, I wrote, 'My girlfriend said this gun is really smooth and easy to use. She was able to shoot my wife several times from fifty feet away.' Laughing, he said, "that one got me banned from Amazon."

Mr. Awesome laughed as well and began to get mentally stimulated.

"Some other ones I did tonight: 'These socks are superthick and absorbant and you can easily jerk off into them for a few weeks before washing them.' They gave me a warning on that one. Want to try one?"

Mr. Awesome's eyes lit up like a Christmas tree. Eddie handed him the laptop. Mr. Awesome scrolled through Amazon, looking for some ideas. He settled on the hat section.

He wrote, "My ugly bald friend loves this hat. He says it's lightweight and fits perfectly on his head. He has to wear hats because the idiot has no hair. He's so repulsive when he doesn't have this magnificent lightweight hat on."

They waited a few minutes, and the review got published.

"Well, Mr. Awesome, usually when they publish the review, that means it's not extreme enough. But it was your first time. I am confident that if you practice daily, you will get banned all the time."

They both chortled like a couple of buffoons.

"Here's another fun one. You know those websites where there is one of those instant chat things where you can talk to a live person?"

Mr. Awesome nodded his head.

"They can be fun messing with as well. I try to pick large corporations websites instead of a smaller mom-and-pop store since large corporations suck."

Eddie clicked on a website and said, "Now let's look for a 'chat now' button. OK, here it is. So you have to fill in your name and reason, which obviously I make up. Now the fun part. They think I have a question about an order, but really I am going to totally be a jerk. It's pretty amusing."

"'Yeah, my order showed up today, but instead of a book, it was a half-eaten hoagie."

"'Sir, we're really sorry. This has never happened before. Are you able to take a picture?'

"'I can't, no. I ate the hoagie, and it was so rotten, I grew an extra finger. So my boss said I was a gross mutant and fired me. So I had to get a job in the local freak show. Since I travel around from town to town and am rarely home, my girl dumped me. So this half-eaten hoagie really screwed me over. Don't get me wrong; I love hanging out with the freaks, great people, salt of the earth. Just today Pumpkin Paul—he's called that because he tattooed his face to look like a pumpkin—anyway, so Pumpkin Paul knew I was depressed, so he hired this really hot hooker for me.'"

Mr. Awesome was cracking up at this point and said, "You think they're going to respond?"

"Let's see, Mr. Awesome. I will now make my demands.

"Anyway, could you please send me another book and your phone #? Remember, I have six fingers. I can do marvelous things."

They waited to see if she would respond. But there was no response, just "chat session ended."

"Dammit, I wanted her to respond!" uttered Mr. Awesome.

"They rarely respond, man; people are so lame."

Mr. Awesome chuckled some more and said, "See you tomorrow, Edward."

# BLIGHT BUSTERS

They woke up early the next morning and continued to practice with Mikey as well as review possible questions and answers the media might launch at them. They all felt confident in their pinball skills and were actually eager to impress anybody who was willing to watch them. They even started competing among themselves on who could get the highest scores on each machine. Wally had the highest score on *Elvira and the Party Monsters* while Mikey had the highest score on *Rocky and Bullwinkle* and *Popeye*. Eddie constantly told them they were cheating assholes who were only winning because they stole his blow to stay up all night and practice. They ignored the ramblings from the whippersnapper.

Detroit would be where Mr. Awesome introduced Mikey's unique economic idea because of its notoriety in becoming the first American city to go bankrupt. So by starting the campaign there, it would make sense in people's minds. They were taking abandoned warehouses and creating jobs. The American public would relish and rave about the president. Statues of him would be erected. He would pay the architect extra on the side to make sure he looked ripped in the statue. Mr. Awesome would get all the credit, and his approval ratings would climb. He would crack the "top twenty best presidents of all time" list.

The bus ride from Philly to Detroit was nine hours and thirty-five minutes. The bus parked in the warehouse district. Endless abandoned buildings. The rats felt great getting off the bus to finally stretch their legs, and flap their wings.

The building where the event was being held looked dilapidated on the outside like the rest of the buildings, but inside it was a flurry of activity. There was a stage set up where Mr. Awesome would speak and then a row of ten pinball machines to the left of the stage. Behind the stage was where the manufacture of pinball machines was already in progress. Endless shiny metal. Two side-by-side clear fifty-foot containers holding pinball balls looked more like weapons of war than important pieces for a game.

Mikey strolled up to the pinball machines and was taken aback at how much of his idea Mr. Awesome had actually listened to. He was used to politicians lying, but this was exactly what his vision was. There were signs above each pinball machine indicating where the money was being allocated. Mikey looked at the list of signs. Schools. Roads. Parks. Fire Company. Police. Gardens. Basketball Courts. Bike Path. Soup Kitchen. He felt a sense of pride he only felt after finishing a song. Nothing was accomplished yet in the big picture of causing some actual change, and it was very possible nobody would be interested in playing pinball—meaning this was a complete waste of time. But just to make it this far was a victory in his mind.

Eddie, Wally, and Ava walked over to Mikey, and they all congratulated him on the signs.

"The more I conceptualize this, Mikey, the more I start to wonder if the lower and rejected classes of people should be part of the decision making in how society works. We are the ones who sleep on the warehouse floors and rummage through the trash to survive, so our ideas are genuine and sterling. Like, what does some rich upper-class politician know or care about hard rock bottom?"

Ava felt warm and cozy as she was sucked into Wally's ideal world for a minute, only to exit it immediately because reality called.

"Guys, go ahead and start playing pinball. In a few minutes, Mr. Awesome will begin his speech. Once he starts, you will stop playing and listen. When he's done, Mr. Awesome and the press will come over and start asking you guys questions. Good luck."

"It feels so great to be back in Detroit. I have so much respect for this city. A city of fighters. Detroit never gives up. Detroit is a city built on manufacturing, and this is why we are very confident and excited about opening the first pinball manufacturing warehouses here. By starting in Detroit, we're telling the rest of America that manufacturing can come back to America and be successful.

"Now to the specifics. I know the media is buzzing about this idea. An idea by a common citizen of America. But we all believe in it. By manufacturing pinball machines and placing them in bars, grocery stores, movie theaters, and any other stores that want them, we are doing two things. First and foremost, we are creating jobs. Behind me is where the manufacturing of pinball has begun. This has created three hundred jobs already, and as the demand for more and more machines rises, which I firmly believe it will, we will have created thousands and thousands of jobs.

"Then comes the interesting and creative part of pinball manufacturing—something that has never been done before—the people choosing how to spend the money. As you can see, there are signs above each pinball machine. Schools, roads, gardens, police, basketball courts. Every time you play a pinball game, half the money goes toward what's listed on the sign. The other half goes toward paying the workers who are building the machines. So if you're upset about a certain part of your town or city that you believe needs fixed, come play some pinball and raise money for it.

If you see an area of your city not represented—for example, you think libraries deserve more money, and libraries are not listed—you can simply log on to this app, tell it which pinball machine you're playing and how many games, and that money will be allocated toward what you want. Now let's go play some pinball. I have to admit, I am not the greatest at this, so let's focus on some other people playing."

Mr. Awesome and the press all shared a laugh.

*Oh, this is going to be interesting.*

Mr. Awesome walked off the stage and went over to the pinball machines. He started playing, and after a minute he told the press, "I warned you: I am not the greatest. Go ahead and ask some questions of those three guys. They appear to be a bit superior to me."

"So what do you guys do for a living?" asked the reporter.

"We're carpenters," Mikey replied. "We work a lot and have families, so we don't patronize bars much; we can't bring our kids, and having a hangover is completely off the radar with our hectic schedules. When we heard about a pinball gallery opening, something clicked inside of us. It just felt natural and pure. We could bring the family out for something that didn't involve cell phone apps, video game violence, and Pokémon.

Eddie began, "Yeah, finally the government has admitted defeat and failure and are now using ideas from the average Joe, so I like what I am seeing."

Mr. Awesome knew that wasn't part of the script. Sweat danced on his brow.

"This concept is a pleasant surprise," Wally said. "Times are tough, and just when it seemed like all hope was gone, this idea popped out of nowhere, igniting a newfound sense of optimism among the people because we know our money will be spent on important things our cities and towns need, and it's the people who get to decide where the money goes. Like my friend mentioned as well, we also really like how we can bring our kids out, and everybody can have a fun time. Nobody needs to worry about being hungover the following day or having any issues at all, since it's a wholesome activity."

Mr. Awesome began to relax again. Wally stuck to the script 100 percent. He used his hands and spoke with enthusiasm.

After ten minutes of interviews, the event began to take root in mellow vibes. The Rats, with their metal fingers, played pinball in a perpetual groove of righteousness. They made pinball look hip with their relentless attack on the metal ball. It flew around inside the machine, walloping and thumbing everything in its path as the machine rewarded the user with point after point, flashing higher and higher scores. A few people from the media and the general public began playing as well.

Two hours later, the event was over. While walking outside the Piss Rats noticed a woman zigzagging in front of them. Clearly, sobriety was not on her to-do list tonight.

Eddie shouted, "Punk rock! That chick rules, getting wasted while playing pinball. How come I didn't think of that?"

"Well, let me think, Eddie. Most likely because we're being paid one hundred thousand dollars," said Wally.

"It's a rhetorical question, buzzkill."

Wally ignored the guitar player and replayed the day's events in his mind. Even though he was working for the government now, having the people choose where their money would be spent in their city or town was pretty punk rock and was aligned with his personal politics. His body chemistry began changing from gooey gray to nourishing neon.

Mr. Awesome came on the bus an hour later. He looked sunny and gratified. "Boys, that was a great night!"

"We're not boys, asshole," retorted Eddie.

"Shut up and stick to the script next time jerk-off." They both sneaked a smile in.

*What the fuck, they're bros now?*

"So, Rats, Chicago is tomorrow; then it's city after city for the next two months with minimal days off. So get some rest tonight, OK?"

"There's actually a great punk show tonight—cool if we go?" said Mikey, who felt like he was fifteen again, begging and pleading with his dad to let him go to a show and have his curfew extended to eleven thirty so he could see the headlining band.

"That sounds like fun. Let's get dinner beforehand, OK?" said a delighted Mr. Awesome.

"Ava, he can't come with us," protested Mikey. "I mean, sorry, but come on; just think about the consequences."

"He can just dress up, so nobody knows the Piss Rats are BFFs with the president of the United States," Ava said with a chuckle. "I mean, there are endless costumes for this two-month tour."

"Great idea, Ava. Then it's been decided, I will just alter my appearance," said Mr. Awesome.

Mikey was hoping it would be just Eddie and Wally, and then he would try to convince Ava to join them. He constantly told himself Ava was part of the problem as he saw it. A vacant vanilla sheep who only made the world worse. Yet, when he was seeking a more mature conversation or suggestion on something, he would seek her out. Was he thirsty for something besides the immature debauchery that rebel music seemed to provide, albeit loving every second of it—but perhaps something solemn and sober was a nice change of pace? Variety and shit.

They went to Detroit Soul for dinner. A vegan café near the venue.

"This is actually pretty damn good for being just vegetables," commented Mr. Awesome.

"Since you're a carnivore, they gave you the special carnivore meal. Fresh roadkill," said Eddie.

"I knew there was meat in this; vegetables don't taste this good," said a jovial Mr. Awesome.

A younger Wally would have grown five hundred arms and legs and immediately pounced on Mr. Awesome, injecting tons of juicy venom into him for his vegetable comment. Instead, he thought about his high score on *Bram Stoker's Dracula* and how if he could have just hit the last ball into Dracula's eyes, it would have released an extra ball. He loved playing when there were two balls active simultaneously, as it really cranked up the intensity of the old-school game.

As they walked to the venue, the Rats all joked about Mr. Awesome's clothes. He looked like their dad or somebody who belonged more at a play or symphony than a punk show.

The Rats ordered Pabst Blue Ribbon pounders, while Mr. Awesome ordered a wheat beer along with shots for everyone. *Sober to buzzed in fifteen minutes*, thought Eddie. *That's my kind of evening.*

Atrocity Solution, Get Dead, Tenement, Small Brown Bike and Iron Chic played before the Lawrence Arms headlined the sold-out show. They were sufficiently tanked and tipsy at this point. Numb and nimble.

After five songs, Eddie yelled to Mr. Awesome, "Want to stage dive?"

Mr. Awesome gave him the thumbs-up signal.

*If Eddie is a real punk, he will find a way to injure Mr. Asshole.*

Wally and Eddie lifted him up on the stage. He adjusted his fake moustache briefly. Then for what felt like an eternity, Mr. Awesome looked out at the group of sweaty, smelly punks dancing to the loud, abrasive sounds. So many thoughts crashed into his skull like a machine gun.

#1: The bold almost cuckoo idea of touring with a punk band and letting them initiate an economic plan.

#2: His wife being so inspired by him listening to a group of punks that she felt all her boxed-up ideas could finally be released as she texted him all day with ideas such as *pay-what-you-can restaurants, changing the top speeds cars can go to forty-five to prevent so many car deaths, free HIV testing kits in all stores, and free DUI breathalyzer key chains.*

#3: His vice president sitting on his chair while he was gone. He told the VP countless times, his chair was molded strictly for his own butt, and when somebody else's butt used it, it totally became less comfortable.

Finally, he leaped into the crowd. Ten thousand fingers supported him. He felt truly liberated and free.

Walking out of the venue, Ava jumped on Mikey's back. She kissed his cheek and screamed, "My ears are ringing!" Then she ran down the street, jumping on various benches and curbs.

*What the fuck was that?* thought Mikey. *She's probably just drunk. Most likely her first concert. She's so lame.* He reached into his sweaty jeans for his cigs. Each inhale of vitamin N caused more thoughts to blossom about Ava. He tossed the smoke to the ground and crushed it with his boot like it was an innocent ant.

Back on the bus, Mr. Awesome said, "Rats, that was a total blast—holy shit—but we got a busy day tomorrow, so let's just blaze a blunt and wind down."

*Blaze a blunt. Did the fuckin' president just say. "Let's blaze a blunt"?*

As the blunt was passed around, Eddie told a new joke. "So I was over at a friend's house, and I put my beer on his coffee table, and he quickly threw a coaster my way. Told me to use it ASAP. But he will park his forty-thousand-dollar car on the city streets every night where people can sit on it, punch it, kick it. Birds can shit on it. But God forbid I put a beer on his shitty Ikea coffee table." They all laughed.

"Eddie, I sense an Ikea theme in your jokes," commented Mr. Awesome.

"Yeah, I don't know. I guess. Fuck it. Here's another new one. What's up with car crashes? I mean, you accelerate, and then when you see another car, you stop. Pretty fuckin' simple: start, stop. Yet like every minute, there's a crash. If I were interviewing people for jobs, I would ask them how many car accidents they have been in. 'So you want to be the accountant for this fifty-million-dollar company, but you have been in six accidents? You can't stop when you're about to hit a car, but you can be the accountant? Don't think so.'"

They were all thoroughly stoned at this point. Mikey asked Ava if she wanted to hear another Piss Rats song. Her bloodshot eyes and smirk indicated she was up to hearing anything at this moment. He put on, The Drunken Botanist.

Walking through an alley when a lady came to me.
She said her name was the drunken botanist and had a tale for thee.
Every Friday night that drink in hand
Well, it comes from the land and not a white coat man.
Walk through a garden with me and what you will see are plants that can be made into a drink or three
*She is a city crawler*
*Always drinking Yards Brawlers*
*Telling those who do not know*
*What they really should know*

*Whoa, whoa*
Like the two-headed baby and bearded lady
It all comes from the land like that drink in hand
And I never had much interest meeting you in a chemical lab
Where the mouth is dry, and the words don't flow
And all I think about doing is "go, go, go."
*She is a city crawler*
*Always drinking Yards Brawlers*
*Telling those who do not know*
*What they really should know*
*Whoa, whoa*
She said you can always visit but cannot stay
See this house will haunt and hate you, shackle and break
you, make you wish you were not alive
This house will haunt and hate you, shackle and break you,
make you wish you were not alive
You can always come visit but cannot stay
Yeah, yeah, yeah, yeah, yeah, yeah, yeah, yeah
*She is a city crawler*
*Always drinking Yards Brawlers*
*Telling those who do not know*
*What they really should know*
*Whoa whoa*

Never shake hands
Never shake hands
With that white coat, with that white coat
Never shake hands, never shake hands with that white coat,
white coat man
Whoa, whoa, white coat man
Whoa, whoa

No one likes a realist, she said
So she lives inside her own head
She crawls these city streets to tell those who do not know
what they really should know Whoa, whoa

Mikey looked over to Ava, feeling pride from his band's folky, swingy punk song, but Ava was passed out.

# JED

Jed's alarm sang its siren song indicating it was 5:00 a.m. Like a frog, he leaped out of bed, stretching his arms, imagining he was a Stretch Armstrong. He positioned his glasses onto his face and commenced the morning routine.

A tablespoon appeared and then disappeared into the fluffy clouds of coconut oil that would find its new home swishing in Jed's mouth for the next twenty minutes to remove toxins that lollygagged on his gums, as they were a gateway and entrance for toxins to wreak havoc on his body.

He launched the refrigerator door open and extracted kale, spinach, carrots, celery, beets, arugula, and oranges into his Hurom juicer to prepare a healthy morning beverage. Jed then extracted blueberries, pineapple, coconut oil, bananas, and hemp protein powder to dump into his blender for his breakfast protein shake.

Yoga. Bike ride. Sunlamp proceeded.

The knob on his shower then twisted and turned to the coldest possible. This would get the blood circulating as well as activate the brain's "blue spot," which would generate the release of nor-adrenaline to prevent depression.

Jed jogged to his car, hopping and jumping on various objects en route. People were used to his jovial, jolly style but still scruti-nized him as he leaped over trash cans and used people's home stairs as if they were exercise equipment.

Once he reached his car, he took a deep breath in, held it, and released. This was repeated thrice to ensure his body had ample amounts of oxygen.

He put on some jazz to relax him and began the short com-mute to his job as a nutritionist. His first client of the day was suf-fering from digestive problems.

"I just feel bloated and achy in my stomach most days," she said.

Jed's requiem for her was no liquids for an hour after each meal and thirty minutes prior to each meal. Chew each bite of food as much as she could. Then take digestive enzymes. These would reduce the bloating and give her energy because she would ab-sorb the nutrients better. Zinc Carnosine would help promote her stomach lining growth and patch up any ulcers. In the afternoon, she would take a quarter cup of aloe vera on an empty stomach followed by juiced cabbage, celery, and carrots to promote further healing. Curcumin, flaxseed, and hemp seed were also added to her new health regime.

He had two more clients to see the rest of the day. After work, he drove home and hopped on his mountain bike to ride the local trail for an hour. After the magnificent ride, he drank some coco-nut water and then began to prepare dinner for his family.

He cut up a plethora of vegetables and baked a salmon. He had a nice conversation with his family regarding education and the benefits of yoga.

After dinner, he spent time with his kids and then watched some TV with his wife.

# AVA

Ava grew up a daddy's girl. She loved both parents equally, but it was her dad who got her senses heightened, as he showered her constantly with presents. She admired his work ethic and always dreamed of one day having a family and being able to provide for them the same way her dad did for her.

On her sixth birthday, her dad bought her an entire aisle at her favorite doll shop. It was hundreds of dolls. Her friends were envious and dreamed of Ava's parents adopting them. On her tenth birthday, he bought her two Savannah cats—$5,000 for each one. On her sweet-sixteenth birthday, she got a cherry-red 1969 convertible. It was her dream car. She knew it was wrong and terrible, but her father was now her favorite parent. All these wonderful material possessions simply consumed her entire soul.

After graduating from high school, all she wanted was to work in her dad's line of business, but what exactly was his line of business? She and her mom were kept in the dark with only rare rays of light to pass through, just enough for them to theorize about it.

#1: FBI
#2: UFO hunter
#3: A prosthetist, since he was often overheard talking about people missing limbs.
#4: Fisherman, since he was always on his boat.

A few times a month, he would have to go away on business. When they asked what kind of business, he would smile and crack a joke, telling them he didn't have time to explain because he was too busy thinking about what gifts he wanted to buy and give them upon his return. They giggled, and everyone seemed content and happy living the good life.

Ava protested attending college. She just wanted to work in her father's line of business. Whatever that was. He told her he worked hard so she could get a great education and discover and figure out what she wanted to do for a career. Plus, he told her, she wouldn't like his profession because there was a lot of cigar smoking, which was bad for your skin, and Ava was obsessed with her skin looking clear and beautiful. So she went to college, and since she couldn't take her '69 cherry Mustang, she went on a shopping spree on Sky Mall's website. When people saw her dorm room, they asked her what her parents did for a profession. She told them, "Well, you know, my dad doesn't like to talk about it, but he works hard, and we love him so much." Rumors began to spread that her father worked for the Mob or was a gangster or something along those lines.

At a frat party, she met a boy who played football, and they began dating. He would ask her from time to time how her family became so rich, and she would always tell him that she didn't know, but her dad worked very hard, and his hands always had calluses.

One night they were watching *Scarface*, his favorite movie, and he joked that maybe her dad sold drugs or was involved in the Mob. She didn't get upset or slap him or anything. Instead, she thought about it for weeks. She started asking her boyfriend questions about drug dealers and the Mob and watching movies about them as well. It all made sense to her. She instantly became worried for her dad's safety since everybody in those movies eventually died or went to prison. She brainstormed for months about what she could do to protect him. Finally, she concluded that she would need to work in the government where she could pull some strings if necessary.

She majored in political science and graduated at the top of her class. She then got her Master's Degree. Her dad and mom were so proud of her. For graduation, her father wanted to buy her a house, but she told him, no more presents; he needed to be more careful with his money and to start saving for retirement.

# BURN DOWN THE FACTORY

Everyone woke up around 10:00 a.m. from the smell of coffee that permeated the bus. Mikey was craving a vat of the liquid crack. Mr. Awesome mumbled some words, and everyone laughed. "Jeez, sorry, guys. Give me a few minutes to shimmy and shiver the ole brain cells into place"

"Too late, asshole," said Eddie. "I just recorded this and texted it to TMZ. You're toast."

Mr. Awesome threw a creamer at Eddie's head. He eluded it, causing it to hit the wall and make a shallow, whimpering thud.

*Kill me now now now now.*

Around midday, the bus was on the highway to Chicago. Mr. Awesome handed out the itinerary. "OK, Piss Rats, here is the dialogue for today. You guys are going to be college professors. Ava will do her best to make you guys look studious and well-read."

As the bus rolled into Chicago, everyone looked out the windows at the third-largest city in America. The Rats always enjoyed coming to Chicago. The vibe seemed to be more about art than the money. The way it should be.

They got off the bus and stretched their arms and soaked up the free vitamin D. Mr. Awesome was immediately engulfed in security and journalists, so the Rats had to move back into the bus so nobody would notice their connection to the president.

"This sucks," Eddie told Ava. "I need to move my legs and breathe the beautiful Chicago air into my lungs."

Ava barely acknowledged his concern and gave him a look of *you damn punks better not screw this up.*

The Rats began to get dressed up as college professors. Mikey put on a wig, a maroon button-down polo shirt with a plaid tie, and worn blue jeans with a brown pair of dress shoes. Eddie couldn't stop laughing as he put on a University of Illinois sweatshirt with a Cubs baseball hat. Wally dressed like a boring working professional.

The bus drove off so the Rats could enter a different part of the building. When they got inside, Ava showed them the pinball machines, and they began to familiarize themselves with them.

The president was one minute into his speech when chaos erupted like an angry volcano.

Wally ran to see what was happening, and his heart rate began to increase as he saw fifty people dressed in all black begin to scream and shout at the president.

"It's the Chicago anarchists," he yelled toward Mikey and Eddie.

Wally knew the anarchist movement well. This particular branch was well organized and disciplined. This was going to be a symphony of warfare. An internal battle rumbled like a motorcycle inside his stomach. Align himself with a cause and scene he'd supported for decades or continue being an employee of the US government? His brain cells stretched and twisted, synapses collided and crashed, and memories flooded his brain of all the time spent with his fellow anarchists protesting everything under the sun. Seeing his friends get maced by the police and arrested, and spend days in and out of court with their court appointed lawyer. The blood, sweat, and tears. He wondered if his friend Chris was still in jail for refusing to let a truck carrying armaments pass.

Then a frightening thought caused his central nervous system to panic. Was his ex-girlfriend Wendy here? She was a devout anarchist and would certainly be able to identify Wally if any part of his disguise came off, which they were beginning to. They'd spent tons of time together in a few squats back in Philly before they both agreed it was best if she worked on bringing her talent and skills to an anarchist city that needed help, which was Chicago. They loved each other immensely, but the cause was always more important than emotions.

He was jolted from his nostalgia by the sounds of Ava screaming. He took a step back and then looked all around nervously. He saw Ava fighting off two anarchists while Mikey and Eddie ran toward her to help. Wally needed to decide fast. Help his new family, or fight alongside his old family? He then charged forward and attacked the anarchist landing punches all over his body. After his enemy was subdued, he ran over to help Mikey against a larger anarchist. Then, out of the corner of his eye, he saw Mr. Awesome fighting a man with a knife. He ran over but realized he had no idea what he would do now. So he jumped on the anarchist's back and put his hands around his neck like he was going to ride him like a horse. Mr. Awesome then began punching and kicking him until he was domesticated and docile.

"You OK, Mr. Awesome?"

"I am OK, thanks, Wally." They let their guard down momentarily, and were quickly surrounded on all sides. Was their demise about to go down?

"Everyone just calm down. Listen, I can give each of you ten thousand dollars if you just drop your weapons and retreat to your homes," said a trembling president. Apparently, Mr. Awesome didn't realize anarchists wouldn't just walk away when presented with money. If they did, they might as well just remove the black clothes and nihilistic thoughts and replace it with khakis and lots of smiles.

"We don't need your money, you filthy slimeball," hissed a tall woman with a nose ring. "We demand that you abandon this materialism and childish pinball venture. It is only causing more suffering and pain for the impoverished people in third world countries who need to produce all the pieces necessary for your game."

An undaunted Wally spoke before Mr. Awesome had time. He needed to be very careful they didn't recognize his voice, so he spoke loudly.

"You have a point. Sure, most likely the pieces are produced in China where the conditions are revolting, but you can never wipe out this system. You have to choose between the best of two evils. So in this case, it's either having the people decide where to allocate the funds or the politicians. Seems to me, it's an easy choice. Pinball wins. Hands down." He was now talking faster and louder. "This is a no-brainer, guys. Go protest something else, anything else, but definitely don't protest this. This could be the seed that, if nurtured and loved, grows into a movement of having the people decide where the money gets allocated. Sure, it's not perfect, and yeah, there's a lot of money being thrown around, but this setup is the best going."

His speech made them even angrier. Their hearts began beating as fast as a hummingbird's; it made the floors shake and flutter, throwing off Mr. Awesome's and Wally's equilibrium. The anarchists began to attack when suddenly a woman appeared, telling them to retreat. Mr. Awesome and Wally looked at each other in bewilderment.

Secret Service finally swooped in to subdue the waves of black that washed in, hoping to create a tsunami. Their angry sea was successful in getting salt in people's eyes, but beyond that, their mission of turning the building into thousands of individual bricks was halted and hindered.

Back on the bus, a frazzled president prudently quizzed everybody on their condition. "Does anybody need medical attention?"

"Fuck that. I channeled the strength and pugnacity of Zeus. Another few minutes, and there would have been piles of bodies," said a confident Eddie.

Everybody, used to Eddie's shenanigans, ignored him and turned inward, pensively reviewing the day's events as well as their bodies for scratches and scars.

*Ha, got what ya traitors deserve. I just wish you had lost.*

The realization of the situation they faced in the coming months hit like a cold cloth. This would not be one big party. There would be battles with punks, agitators, black sheep, and loose cannons who didn't see eye to eye with pinball manufacturing. The Piss Rats would have to dig deep inside and pick a side. Tonight they picked the side they'd stood opposite from for most their lives. Would they have the endurance to pick that side again?

Around 11:00 p.m., when everything and everyone was mellowed out, the Rats, Ava, and the president met in the living area of the bus. Mr. Awesome suggested smoking some weed before bedtime. Everyone haphazardly agreed. Nobody said much. Too exhausted from the day's events.

Mikey got high and let his mind wander. It darted back and forth like a squirrel in the road, finally settling on Johnny Piss Rat. Where the hell was he? Mikey thought about how he first met Johnny.

It was in ninth grade, and Mikey's commencement into punk rock was under way. He lugged compact discs of the normal suspects in his book bag. Rancid, Bad Religion, Crass, NOFX, Face to Face, Ten Foot Pole, Bad Brains, Dead Kennedys, Minor Threat, Lagwagon, Social Distortion and the Mighty Mighty Bosstones. It was seventh period, and time to perform experiments in science class. He leisurely toddled over to his group, dreading the mundane process that awaited. He put on his apron and safety glasses, and when he went to grab his bag, he miscalculated because of the murky glasses and tilted the bag, spilling out his Pennywise CD. Rob, the tall, slender athletic jock in his group, picked it up. He quickly visually inspected it. If history taught Mikey anything, it was that Rob would make fun of him or toss the CD in the trash. Instead, his mouth moved, yielding a sentence that surprised Mikey.

"My brother Johnny has this CD as well. You two are probably the only ones in this school who listen to this type of music; you guys should hang out."

Mikey nodded and mumbled, "Yeah, cool, man."

The following week in science class, Rob came up to Mike and said, "Hey, my brother said you should meet him after school in the parking lot. He has a few CDs he wants you to listen to."

Mikey's heart raced a bit. He didn't really have any close friends, so his brain hastily and inappropriately pictured them becoming best buds till the end of time.

Three p.m. finally arrived, and Mikey began the short trek to the parking lot. A teacher tried stopping him to discuss his performance in class, and he simply swatted at them like a feral fly, trying to seek refuge on a hot meal. He had no patience for the teacher's asinine malarkey. He spotted Rob's brother perched on his trunk, sucking in delicious and toxic cigarette smoke.

"Hey, your brother mentioned you dig some of the same tunes," said an animated Mikey.

"Oh yeah, man; punk rules. Check out these gems." He handed Mikey Avail and the Bouncing Souls and then hopped off his trunk like a badass bunny and said, "Let me know what you think." And in the blink of an eye, the encounter was over.

All of Mikey's energy was put into his left leg to ensure it stayed on the accelerator. He busted through a red light, hitting a squirrel and clipping a car's rearview window. That didn't slow him down as he ran a biker off the road into a ditch, where he saw his skull crack open like an egg leaking yolk. He was shaken from his fantasyland by the driver beeping his horn behind him, and Mikey gently moved his car down the lane to avoid any speeding tickets. He opened his front door and scampered up to his room to eagerly listen to Avail's "Dixie" and the Bouncing Souls' "The Good, the Bad, and the Argyle." After he listened to both albums, Mikey immediately wanted to find Johnny and tell him how wicked they were. But it was Friday—two and half days until Monday landed when he could speak with Johnny. He could barely contain his excitement. He wanted to lend Johnny some CDs on Monday to show his dedication to punk. He looked at his CDs. Not many. A few dozen. He asked his mom if she could take him to one of the record stores in his area. She agreed, and he picked up three new CDs. He spent most of the weekend listening to his new CDs as well as his old ones.

On Monday he found Johnny at lunch and said, "Hey, man, those CDs were fucking awesome. Here are a few I like."

They began trading CDs every week and then retreating into their rooms at home, listening to them nonstop. Reading every lyric. Looking at every part of the CD. The artwork, the thank-you lists, the actual CD. Finally, after a month, Johnny said, "Hey, man, wanna come over tonight? My parents are out for the evening."

Mikey went over around 6:00 p.m. with a book bag filled with every CD he owned and a rare optimistic outlook. They ate pizza and drank Coke while never letting more than a few minutes of silence occur between changing albums. It was a substantially bountiful Friday night, producing a new friendship that saw them going to local shows and hanging out almost every day.

One day at school, while at lunch, a few football players body-checked Mikey and Johnny while they were walking to their table, and their food went flying. The football players began dying of laughter. Everyone in the lunchroom noticed and began laughing as well.

Mikey was hanging out at Johnny's house after school when Rob came up to them and said, "Hey, guys, sorry about what happened at lunch. Those guys are assholes."

"Yeah, whatever," they said and ignored the football player, whom they associated with being just another jock who gave them shit. Feeling even worse now, Rob said, "Fuck that shit. They mess with family, they mess with me. Listen, I know I am on the football team with those guys, but what they did earlier was bullshit. Let's get some revenge."

So began Mikey and Johnny's careers as pranksters. Rob would give them inside information, and Mikey and Johnny would design a prank. The first one was on two football players. Rob knew from a drunken night that one of them slept with a teddy bear while the other one wore Teenage Mutant Ninja Turtle pajamas. So Rob sneaked over at night to take pictures of the two. If he was caught, he could just laugh it up and say, "Oh, it's just some football stuff I am doing." Then the parents, in love with football, would say, "No problem, Rob; just make sure ya have a great game this Friday night."

With no regret or hesitation, Rob dispensed the pictures to Mikey and Johnny. They spent a few days pondering their course of action. What would inflict maximum embarrassment? They finally settled on hanging the pictures all around school with the words "touch guys?" under them. The football players went apeshit, vowing to rupture and gash the guilty parties.

The future Piss Rats loved it. They didn't feel one ounce of guilt. They procured Rob for more inside information. He was reluctant at first. This was just a once-and-done thing. But as Rob noticed the two outcasts getting picked on more and more, he told himself that until they were free from the shackles and chains the jocks locked on them, he would continue to provide them with ammo.

The next lucky victim was the soccer captain. Rob told them that at the end of lunch, he would always, without fail, use the restroom for a few minutes. Rob then left the rest up to them to see what they could come up with, as he was curious to see what type of plan their minds would produce. Three days later, he saw one of the funniest things in his life. The soccer captain was running down the hall, crying, covered in blue paint.

That evening Rob saw the two and fell to the floor laughing. "Holy shit, was that funny. Ruthless as hell, but hey, he deserved it, right? I saw him call you freaks in front of everyone last week."

"Yeah, fuck him," said Johnny. "What else ya got?"

And so began endless pranks and jokes on those people who'd initiated the war. The Piss Rats simply finished the war, and they always won. Eventually, they recruited a couple of other punks and decided to start the Piss Rats after they had pranked almost every jerk in the school.

"Mikey—hey, Mikey, you OK?" asked Wally.

"Oh shit. Hey, sorry, man. I was just thinking about Johnny, guys. I really miss him and worry about him. I'm going to call Carla again tomorrow to see if she's heard from him and see what's going on."

They all revealed to Mr. Awesome how meaningful Johnny was in their lives. Mr. Awesome listened to their stories and then said good night. As he walked back to his makeshift room on the bus, a strong wave of empathy rolled across him. He paused and then reached inside his gut, removing the empathy. He held it up to his eyes, blinking a total of thirteen times. He glanced at his trash can and then his dresser. He sat on his bed, blinking his eyes over and over before retiring for the evening.

# SCHUYLKILL SLOTHS

They awoke the next morning sore but rested and focused. Glad that everyone had survived their first major speed bump. They seemed closer and ready to ignite a flame to burn down anybody in their path.

"OK, Rats, let's put Chicago behind us and prepare for Minneapolis."

En route to Minneapolis, Ava gave them their new assignments. They all worked for the park services in charge of the ten thousand lakes.

"This ain't too bad," said Wally.

"Are there really ten thousand lakes?" questioned Eddie. "I have a feeling they're exaggerating a bit, ya know?"

"Eleven thousand, eight hundred forty-two lakes," said Mikey, using his smartphone quickly, as he was also curious himself.

"Damn," said Eddie.

They looked over their dialogue. Looked simple enough.

*If the Piss Rats were true punks, they would tie up Mr. Asshole and toss him in one of those lakes.*

They got to the warehouse at 4:00 p.m. The event was to begin around 7:00 p.m. They had some time to kill, so they walked around Minneapolis and eventually decided to eat at Galactic Pizza. The Rats ordered three vegan pizza's with tons of toppings.

"This is pretty good for being vegan," commented Ava.

"It's the brick oven," said Wally, a vegan pizza enthusiast. "They just destroy all other pizza ovens."

"Let's stop at the Triple Rock Social Club to see if anybody from Dillinger Four is there," said Eddie.

"Unfortunately Eddie, we can't do that. How would we explain ourselves? That we just happen to all be in Minnesota not on tour and missing our singer? To suspicious," said Mikey.

Wally aggressively scratches his arm so his brain could focus on the piercing pain instead of thinking about missing a drinking session with the legendary Dillinger Four.

They went back to the factory and got dressed for the event on the bus. They all wore overalls with baseball hats. Mr. Awesome's speech was basically identical to the ones in the past, adding a new line about how when it's negative twenty outside, wouldn't they love to be inside playing pinball? Then the reporters interviewed the Rats while they played pinball. Their steel-laced fingers played endlessly like a player piano while discussing the positive virtues of pinball. As the night was winding down, they noticed a man stumbling after finishing a long pinball game. Security promptly removed him.

"Hey, did you notice that guy who looked all messed up after the pinball game?" asked Eddie.

"Yeah, kinda reminded me of Detroit where that lady was fucked up afterward," said Mikey.

"Mikey, what's your opinion? You grew up playing pinball. Did anybody ever get all dizzy and whatnot after playing?" said Wally.

"Not that I can recall, no. America is a lot unhealthier than back in the eighties and nineties though. So many people on meds now. They're also consuming so much shitty GMO food while playing on their phones or gadgets instead of exercising, so maybe with how the ball goes back and forth and up and down, it causes their equilibrium to be off, resulting in a case of vertigo?"

"But I haven't seen Eddie have any issues, and he's a walking drugstore that leaks green toxic radiation when he sweats," expressed Wally.

"So funny you are, Wally. A modern-day Don Rickles."

"Eddie, I am not trying to be funny. There is green sludge leaking out of your eyes right now—don't you feel it?"

Eddie knew there wasn't green sludge leaking from his eyes, but Wally usually was so serious and lacking any sense of humor, so perhaps he was telling the truth. Eddie walked away and then reached up, feeling his face for any toxic waste.

That evening, Mr. Awesome was in a particularly feisty mood. "Goddamn, that speech went smooth," he said. "I really think this pinball crap is going to catch fire." Then he disappeared for the rest of the evening. They could hear him calling a few different people and talking to them for a lengthy time.

The Rats hung with Ava and watched TV for the rest of the night. They worked on a few new songs on their acoustic guitars while Wally tapped on a few books as makeshift drums.

Eddie felt a buzz in his pants. He looked down and noticed the mustard stain on his jeans. It had been there for two days now. He thought about cleaning it up and then said fuck it. His pants continued buzzing. It was probably his wife, Clash, sending a transmission signal to him that said, "Mess this up, and I will bite you like a vampire." *Screw her*, he thought and quickly regretted thinking that. He loved her, but he was sick and tired of everyone around him losing morals and ethics once an opportunity for money arose.

He thought about his former band, the Schuylkill Sloths. No way would they have joined forces with the president just for money. They would have told the president to fuck off or agreed to help him and then totally embarrassed him while taking the money and spending it all before he could retrieve it. The Sloths were totally deranged, frantic, and unhinged. They wrote only twelve songs and would play only secret shows and never once did an interview. They had no online presence at all. They broke up after just two years. They were punk as fuck, the way it should be. The older, mature Eddie told himself that the manufacturing of pinball would help out society and the money would help him and his wife. He felt like he finally understood the Descendents song about not wanting to grow up.

# NOTHING FITS

Jed woke up the next morning feeling optimistic and effervescent. Lickety-split, the vibe went astray when he slid his feet into his shoes and his toes crunched into the top of them before his heel had a chance to get all snuggled in. Confused and perplexed, he put on another pair of shoes, and the same affliction hindered his morning routine. He attempted to clear up this tangled nonsense by walking around in them while getting ready for work. But the sensation of pain and annoyance would not go away. He would have to wear his flip-flops, and if anybody questioned him, he would comment, "Nasty blisters from a pair of new running shoes. You don't want to see it; trust me."

He then put on his dress pants, and they stopped short of his ankles by a few inches. His dress shirt was the same. Starting to panic a bit, he rushed to find his wife.

"Patti, I am freaking out right now. None of my clothes fit me!"

She inspected him up and down like the police investigating a suspect. "Well, I can't see anything noticeable. Put on your work clothes, and let's see."

As he began to take off his dress clothes and put on his work clothes, his kids could be heard running around downstairs, going apeshit instead of being orderly and civil and mentally preparing for the day like he'd taught them.

With the kids out the door into the fascinating, albeit perplexing strange world that had the tenacity to show no remorse or sorrow to anybody, Jed and Patti were alone to analyze the troubling situation.

"The clothes I can understand; they can shrink. But all my shoes?" said a puzzled Jed.

"This just makes no sense at all," said a twitchy Patti.

Jed went into his closet and proceeded to try on every article of clothing. The bigger, baggier clothes still fit, but the ones that fit just right before were now a thing of the past.

"Well, let's discuss this tonight; we're both late for work," said a nervous Patti.

Work crawled by slower than a stoned slug. Finally, when the finish line appeared, they both raced home to further investigate the morning's strange situation that hung around like morning fog on their radar all day.

"So I was thinking: I wonder if it's one of the supplements I take that's causing me to grow," said Jed.

"Well, yeah, that would make sense, but the problem with that theory is that people stop growing in their late teenage years. At the latest, in their early twenties. High levels of sex hormones, primarily estrogen, released after puberty cause the bones' growth plates to close. If anything, you should be downsizing," said Patti.

"This is just so bizarre. Let's give it some time and see what happens," said Jed.

# BRIGHT EYES

They left for Wisconsin in the morning. The mood was dry, stale, and crusty, like a piece of aged bread. Nothing was particularly wrong. Everybody was getting along just fine, the events were successful, and the mainstream media was reporting on it positively, but everybody was missing home and tired from the long days and longer nights of partying.

The Rats were dressed up as security officers from a local pharmaceutical company. Eddie discussed all the pills he would steal if he really did work security there.

"See, what I would do is pretty simple. During a storm, I would pull the power plug on the main electrical outlet. This would short-circuit the cameras. Then I would start taking pills. Oxy, of course. Morphine. Percocet, Viagra."

Wally couldn't take any more from the delusional punk and told him to just shut up. "You would never actually do that."

Eddie fought the urge to throw something at him and just said, "Sorry, Wally; next time I will just talk about vegan pizza to make you jubilant."

"You can talk about anything you want, Eddie, but just be a little realistic. I mean, come on; you wouldn't really do what you just said. That's a felony. Meaning jail. Meaning no more Clash and no more music. You would chicken out."

Eddie walked away and grabbed his phone to text his wife, asking her how his record collection was doing. Was she keeping the AC on so the records stayed legit? He also told her how much he missed her stunning bright eyes.

Growing up, Eddie had been a rambunctious kid. A bouncy ball who never stopped bouncing. His parents and teachers could never quite figure out how to calm him down. They tried sports. But Eddie would just frustrate his coach and team with endless questions, comments, and remarks about the game he was supposed to be playing instead of actually playing the game. They tried art. But Eddie would just dump all the paint on the canvas and proudly proclaim it "art." Out of solutions, his father decided Eddie would just have to hang out with him until something clicked and could focus the boy.

One Saturday afternoon in the spring, his father put on a NASCAR race and cracked open a beer.

Eddie was on the couch and asked his father, "What are those cars doing?"

His father replied, "They're racing, son. Whoever goes around the laps four hundred times the fastest is the winner."

Eddie said, "Oh, OK."

With nothing better to do, he continued watching the cars fly by at warp speed around the track. The speed of the cars matched his raw and primal urges. When he discovered race car driving, he felt he could live vicariously through the cars. When he felt like he was about to explode, his mind retrieved memories of the latest race he watched, and he felt oddly calm. When it was discovered in school that he spent most of his time watching race cars with his father, he was ruthlessly attacked by the other middle school kids who said he was white trash and a hick for loving race cars.

Unable to take the verbal abuse anymore, he quit watching or thinking about race cars. But without them, he began to act out in school. During lunch, he would spray ketchup on his shirt and pretend he was shot. When teachers asked him anything, he would respond with "*Que?*" In gym class, when they played dodgeball, he would only throw the ball at the gym teacher's face. He was out of control without his race cars.

When he first heard Subhumans' The Day the Country Died, he finally felt at peace with the world. He directed all his energy toward dressing like a punk and listening to the heaviest, fastest, angriest punk out there. Discharge and Black Flag were his foundations. He got picked on even more aggressively than before, but he didn't care. He absolutely loved the music. Every time the jocks gave him shit about his Mohawk, he vowed to make it even taller and brighter the following day.

# FAMILY

When they got to Wisconsin, they noticed a pinball game standing out from the pack of normal ones. *Ripley's Believe It or Not, Sopranos, Monopoly, Elvira and the Party Monsters, Cirqus Voltaire,* and *The Piss Rats.*

They started freaking out. The graphics included their faces with Mohawks. Then all round the machine were pictures of rats, guitars, booze, and skulls.

"This is so damn cool, wow," said Wally.

"Wally, they captured your long nose just perfectly," said Eddie.

"Yeah, well, they captured your double chin and huge forehead just perfectly too," said Wally.

Mr. Awesome sauntered over, and they thanked him a million times.

"Guys, I wanted to do something special. I know we don't see eye to eye on a lot of stuff, and we are basically from different planets, but I wanted to show my gratitude to you guys for actually making this fun for me. It's really stressful being president, and you guys could have just gone on autopilot, but you didn't, so thanks."

*Ahhhh isn't this so cute. The Piss Rats and the president and the president's assistant are one big happy family now. Just the way the Ramones pictured it I am sure.*

Again they noticed somebody finishing a pinball game, looking confused and dazed. Security removed the person again.

"Guys," said Mikey, "I think I am noticing a trend here. Except for Chicago, a person finishes a pinball game, and he or she looks and acts all fucked up. And I bet if there weren't a riot in Chicago, we would have seen off-balanced humans there as well."

Ava came in and sat close to Mikey. He quickly changed the subject to what they were going to do tonight. Ava suggested bar-hopping, and they all agreed.

They found a local bar and began drinking. Mikey asked Mr. Awesome how the media and public were reacting to the manu-facturing of pinball machines to spur growth in the economy. Mr. Awesome took a long swig, smiled wide, and said, "It's going pretty good, Mikey. I really think your idea is taking off." He put his fist out for a fist bump for Mikey, and everyone started laughing.

"Now, some economists from quack independent media com-panies are saying it will take years and years for this to make any money or help the economy, if it does at all, but luckily, they are not from the mainstream media, so their thoughts won't gain any traction."

*Shit*, Mikey thought, what if it were true, and his idea was just a dud? He tried to ask Mr. Awesome follow-up questions the rest of the night, but Mr. Awesome wasn't entirely interested in answering them honestly it seemed. He just kept telling Mikey, "Listen, everyone has the right to their own opinion. First Amendment. Just because a few people say pinball won't create job growth and help out local econo-mies with money for various things, doesn't mean they're correct. My team says it will help out. So don't worry or sweat it. Just focus on getting your dialogue correct and playing pinball at the rallies."

*It's a good idea, Mikey, but when the government gets involved, it's usually done wrong. I hope Mikey will keep an eye on everything to make sure there's no corruption happening. Which most likely there will be, since it involves government and money.*

As the night progressed, Mr. Awesome's swashbuckling got larger and larger. He was slamming beer and shots and just acting like a total asshole. When Eddie told him the song he'd selected on the jukebox was fuckin' lame, Mr. Awesome grabbed Eddie and told him he could make the punk disappear. Here now, gone tomorrow. This left a sour taste in Eddie's mouth. He told the Rats what had happened, and like an army, they retreated back to the bus.

Ava and Mr. Awesome showed up an hour later. Mr. Awesome stumbled in and told the Rats punk rock was fuckin' dumb and then tried to hook up with Ava. She slapped him and told him to get some sleep.

"Wow, I am so sorry, guys. He is completely wasted," said Ava.

"Ava, he told me he could make me disappear in an instant. What the fuck?"

"Eddie, don't worry. You are fine."

"Fuck you, Ava. In case you haven't noticed, the singer of our band has disappeared, so sorry if I am a little paranoid right now."

"Eddie, Johnny's disappearance has zero to do with Mr. Awesome. Mr. Awesome has never made a person vanish; he just let his ego and booze control him tonight. The president is in a very stressful position, and he's taking a huge gamble in spending all this time and resources on pinball. Let's just call it a night. There's still a long time left on the road."

As Mikey was brushing his teeth, he caught a glimpse of Ava changing into sweatpants. *Those legs*, he thought. He finished brushing his teeth and pretended he needed some water. He looked at Ava, who looked back.

"Important to stay hydrated," said Mikey.

"Yeah, it is. So, Mikey, what do you think actually happened to Johnny?"

Mikey thought, *Shit, does Ava know something? Does she think Mr. Awesome is connected to Johnny becoming invisible?*

"I have no clue, Ava. Johnny really had no enemies. I mean, could the jocks in high school have found out we committed all those pranks and finally had their revenge? I really don't know. I mean, kidnapping him just because we committed some pranks in high school seems really extreme."

"I agree, Mikey. I can't imagine it's that, but perhaps it could be. Maybe they found out and got drunk, and well, this is 2017. Stuff like this happens daily."

Mike began to get nervous at the thought of his best friend, Johnny, being duct-taped and tied to a chair in a basement while the jocks took their revenge on him. His face began to show some tension as a feeling of anguish and uneasiness swept through his body.

Ava noticed this and gave him a hug and then a kiss on his cheek and said, "I really hope Johnny turns up." And then she walked to her bedroom.

# POLITICIANS ON A HOLIDAY

Mikey woke up thinking about Johnny and the pranks they pulled in high school. When the Piss Rats started getting more popular, they'd slowed down on their pranks and spent more time learning their instruments. He thought about how much of an asshole Mr. Awesome was last night and began thinking about a prank they could pull on him.

He texted his bandmates: "Let's prank Mr. Awesome like the good ol' days. Also, let's design the prank to pry information from him about what's really happening with people being escorted out after playing pinball."

Two seconds later, Eddie replied, "Sounds good."

Wally confidently countered with: "Let's make this a great prank."

Mikey felt stupid for texting them when they were just a few feet away.

Colorado was up next. The Rats were finally allowed to dress somewhat normal. They were owners of a Weed Café. Ava came in to deliver the dialogue, which was basically identical to Wisconsin. They were tired of bars and looking for something a little different after work, especially since they were around pot all day. They wanted a different vibe, and pinball fit that niche nicely. As the event was closing down, it looked like a dozen people were fucked up. Security removed them all.

"Well, what a surprise," said Wally. "Somebody is fucked up after pinball."

"Yeah, well, this is Colorado," said Mikey.

"Weed doesn't make you that fucked up," said Eddie.

"Who knows, maybe the back and forth of the ball plus the fact that it's Colorado and most people are high, makes them dizzy," said Mikey.

As they were leaving, a reporter stopped the Rats and said, "I saw you boys get off the bus that the president of the United States was on. Are you working with him?"

"His name is Mr. Awesome," Eddie said. He grabbed the microphone and pretended to perform oral sex on it, totally grossing the reporter out and making her run away. Eddie yelled, "Don't fuck with pinball punks!"

Eddie saw a wooded area and some train tracks and decided to take a walk back there. He could use a few minutes of solitude. He decided to work on a new joke he'd been thinking about.

"You ever noticed how happy and excited everyone is when they find out you're having a baby, and then, when you have the baby, it's like the greatest thing in the world? But the reality is, they're basically saying, 'hey, we're so glad and happy for you that you now will have to spend most of your time and money on a child who will most likely hate you or not appreciate you until they're in their thirties if they even make it that long.'" *Ugh*, he thought. *Way too depressing and cynical. Also, sounds like something Carlin already did and did much better.* He then decided to work on a new song: "Just a politician on a holiday, will there ever be another way." *It's a catchy chorus*, he thought. He would need a bridge and prechorus and other lyrics as well, which he would work on during the tons of downtime he now had.

*I like the kid joke; it's raw and real. Maybe Eddie will return to it later and try to tweak it.*

"So how did the event go for you guys?" asked Mr. Awesome.

"It went pretty smooth," said Wally, "but I wanted to punch that one reporter in the face. First, she asked if you were delusional or just blind to waste all this precious time and resources promoting something so juvenile as pinball. Then she came over to us and asked if we were having a midlife crisis and shouldn't we be doing something more mature. I seriously was seconds away from slapping that microphone from her. Don't be pissed, Mr. Awesome, but I found out which car was hers and slashed one of her tires. I mean, everybody else is psyched and excited on pinball, and she comes in all fucking ignorant, trying to slow down something positive."

*Wally might not act like the party punk Eddie wants him to be, but he is fiercely loyal and will always fight for what he thinks is right.*

Mr. Awesome walked over and sat next to Wally. He stared into his eyes. Everyone was a little worried. Was he exacerbated or content? "Wally, I truly wish there were more dedicated and serious people like you in the world. When doppelgangers become a safe and trendy procedure, I am going to personally ensure each state gets a Wally or two."

Wally and the others felt a tad strange and odd over Mr. Awesome's awkward comment.

"Just a politician on a holiday, will there ever be another way, hey, hey," sang Eddie gaudily. Everyone gave him a nasty look. "Just practicing a new song. We are a band, you know?"

"Want to catch some dinner?" said Ava, trying to break up the tension caused by Eddie's outburst. They decided on True Food Kitchen.

Mr. Awesome already seemed to be getting fired up. He swatted at his fries like they were Russian spies, and they all sprayed off the table in different directions, hitting the floor. "Need fresh fries," said an arrogant Mr. Awesome.

"Dude, calm down," said Eddie. "Have some respect."

"Eddie, don't tell me how to behave. I am the fuckin' president. I know what I am doing—don't need your two cents."

"Yeah, well, you needed Mikey's suggestion on how to ramp up the economy, so you're not totally correct with that statement.

Mr. Awesome quickly jolted his head. Almost twitching, he scratched his arm and then quietly said, "I just want some fresh fries that are not overcooked." Ava and Mikey looked at each other with expressions of *what the hell is going on lately with Mr. Awesome. Those fries were perfect.*

"Well, we're in Colorado. Is everyone ready to get high?" said the president, who was now in a peppier mood all of a sudden. The Rats and Ava reluctantly agreed, hoping Mr. Awesome would conduct himself worthier.

*Please, God, let me get high and stay high till death.*

After ten minutes at the first weed joint, everyone was super stoned and could not stop laughing. Ava felt like an owl as she moved her neck to look at Mr. Awesome. His smirk and delighted disposition were welcomed and accepted. Was this a good time to toss some two cents into the ring and see if it survived? She kept thinking about how owls move their necks 360 degrees and how she could have just sworn her own neck did the same. To avoid getting deeper in the rabbit hole, she risked upsetting the president with some reality.

"So, Mr. Awesome, how are we feeling?"

"I am so fuckin' baked right now." He then proceeded to play air guitar even though there was no music playing.

"So let's try to act cordial tonight, OK?"

"Yeah, Ava, not sure what's been happening to me lately. Maybe just the stress of being away from my family and kids. I miss them so much."

"That's perfectly normal, Mr. Awesome. You can always talk to me about your problems."

He said, "Thanks, Ava," and put his hand on her thigh. She looked a little annoyed at this after he'd just commented on missing his family.

They went to two other cafés and proceeded to get so high they could barely walk. It felt like their muscles had been replaced by fluffy white clouds and their brains were now kaleidoscopes. Ava and Mikey would gaze at each other trying to communicate but their surroundings would swivel and saunter, generating booming and whooping smiles and giggles instead of coherent dialogue.

"So you think Mikey and Ava are going to hook up," said Eddie.

"Yeah, I doubt it, man. He's a punk, and she's the president's assistant," said a stoned Wally.

"So who cares? He doesn't have to marry her."

Wally tried not to be disappointed in Eddie's attitude toward women, and after ten seconds he was already mentally drifting away, thinking about the beautiful pipe they had just smoked out of. He wondered how hard it was to blow glass into pipes. Did one go to school for it? They sure were gorgeous pipes. Would he start smoking weed just for the sublime pipes and bongs? He had enough money where he could buy them and present them as art or stick flowers in them if he didn't want to become a pothead. He then started cracking up, laughing at his thoughts. Always so anti-drug, and now he was daydreaming about weed pipes.

# TIMES ARE TOUGH STICK TOGETHER TILL WE'VE HAD ENOUGH

"Wally, clean your room!" said his mom. "Why is your room always so messy? Are you protesting me, Wally? Why, why, why would you do this? Your mother loves you, Wally!" said his mom.

"Mom, my room is perfectly clean. In fact, it can't get any cleaner!" Wally slammed his door shut and tried to resist crying. He knew his mom had some mental issues and she really was trying to be a great mom, but he sensed she was losing the battle. He never knew what she was afflicted with, but her condition required many bottles with caps that were designed for children of his age to have trouble opening.

His dad was a major league baseball pitcher and always on the road, so they hired a live-in maid. Her name was Alice, and she loved to smoke and teach Wally about the world via aphorisms.

"Walter," she would always say, "life is fresh and vibrant like an apple on a branch, but when that apple is picked, it eventually will become rotten."

"Walter, see this cigarette, and now see the smoke it produces? We humans are the cigarettes, and the government makes us produce smoke—so much smoke, our cigarettes burn down to nothing."

Wally lived near the train tracks and started spending more and more of his time alone down there or with the neighborhood kids. On the train tracks, he didn't have to worry about his mom or Alice, or wonder about which city his dad he rarely saw was in.

One day, while hanging on the tracks, he saw somebody hop off a freight train. They looked at each other, and the guy asked Wally what town he was in. Wally told him, and the man said, "Thanks," and then inquired where the bus station was. Wally examined him. Dark clothes with acres of dirt that made him look like a walking oil spill. His hair was twisted, which Wally would later learn was called dreadlocks. And all over his clothes were patches with what seemed to be band names on them. Seeking an adventure and a break from his normal routine, Wally told the counterculture guy to follow him. They began their long journey on a crisp fall afternoon.

Wally asked the guy why he hopped off the train. The guy, named Sluggo, said it's just what he did. He hopped on and off trains, then sometimes took a bus somewhere. He didn't believe in working or paying rent. Wally was confused. "So you're able to survive living this way?"

"Yeah," said Sluggo. "It's not an easy life, though. It gets cold, hot. I get hungry and tired, but I just can't work a job all week and then use the majority of that money for bills. See, kid, the rich just use us to make them money; we're pawns in their crooked chess game."

They walked the next mile without talking. Wally thought about life without his mom and her disease, without Alice and her smoking and weird one-liners about life and his major league baseball dad who was never around, and he honestly felt his life would be better without them. He told Sluggo he might want to live his lifestyle. Sluggo told him to finish high school first.

"See, the older you get, kid, the wiser you become. So sure my lifestyle looks ideal now, but maybe down the road, it might not be what you want. What I am trying to basically say is, just finish high school first. Find some friends who share in your hobbies, and try to have fun. Unfortunately, if you choose punk, you will be battling authority figures and jocks and mainstream crap most of your life. After high school, then you can decide what path to travel."

Wally thought, *That does make sense.* Sluggo then gave him two cassettes before they parted ways. Operation Ivy and Sex Pistols. Sluggo said, "Kid, I see myself in you, and I know life is rough, but these two albums gave me some kind of hope. Hope to at least not give up and to always do what I find necessary for my soul."

Wally fell in love with those three tapes. Listened to them endlessly. When he eventually met up with Mikey and Johnny for the first time, he said, "God Save the Wally." They looked at him oddly and asked if he liked the Sex Pistols too and did he want to start a band. The last few lines was how he told the story sometimes to naive people when asked how the band started.

# MOUNTAIN PUNKS

Utah was up next. The drive from Colorado through Utah was divine and ravishing. The mountains were soaring and tremendous. Still feeling the residential effects of pot on their brains, the Piss Rats imagined playing a show on the top of a mountain. They pictured it being advertised as "The Greatest Punk Show on Earth." Anytime they noticed a racist or jerk, the band would stop playing and toss that person off the mountain while everybody cheered their death. At the end of the show, the praise for their artistic endeavors would be never ending, and they would be proclaimed the most forward-thinking punk band of the modern age. The Rats' daydreaming was interrupted by Mr. Awesome handing out their next assignments. They were going to be truck drivers.

"So I wonder if Mr. Awesome is going to be a weird asshole again," said Mikey.

"Yeah, what's up with that? He was pretty cool up until a few nights ago," said Eddie.

They arrived in Utah around 4:00 p.m. The building was an old ironworks facility. Mr. Awesome gave his speech, and they then interviewed the Rats.

A woman was playing pinball next to Eddie, and she seemed to sway back and forth, holding on to the machine as an anchor.

Wally saw a man in his mid twenties remove his shirt while sweating profusely.

*Sweaty, hairy, overweight guys should never remove their shirts in public.*

After the event, the Rats got on the bus and cracked open some beers.

"Did anybody see the guy next to me? He took his shirt off and then couldn't stop sweating," said Wally.

"I think some shady shit is going down, guys. At almost every rally, there have been people leaving the pinball games fucked up. We keep asking the same question it seems: Are the pinball machines causing this?" said Eddie.

"That's impossible. It's just a game. They're probably just drinking before they come here. Or smoking some weed or taking pills. Shit, or maybe they're hanging out with Mr. Awesome and taking whatever he's taking," said Wally.

"Should we get Mr. Awesome really fucked up tonight and try to pry some information out of him?" said Mikey.

"Yeah, but he won't drink a ton, knowing he can't afford a crazy hangover tomorrow since we're in the long stretch right now. Rallys are almost daily. We need street drugs. Do they even have street drugs in Utah?" asked Mikey.

"Well, Las Vegas is tomorrow. Let's try to score something then," said Eddie.

*Would be a shame if he OD'd. It really would. Not.*

It was night in Utah, and everyone's bodies felt like they were saturated with sedatives, causing a lethargic attitude to infect them. Mikey sat next to Ava and asked her where Mr. Awesome was.

"Oh, he's in his room listening to Dan Deacon on his headphones."

"Ava, do you think he's taking pills or something? I mean, he's been acting weird, and now he's listening to electronic music on his headphones alone in his room?"

"Yeah, he has been acting weird. It's like a mixture of ego and guilt. I don't know what his deal is. He hasn't said anything is bothering him really. Well, that's not entirely true, Mikey. I did talk to him last night, and he said he missed his family, but then he put his hand on my thigh, so that sort of countered what he'd just said."

Mikey thought about opening the vault to Ava. Telling her of the Rats' plan to spike and dose the president of the United States of America with street drugs to pry out some information, but he had been burned in the past trusting people who at the time seemed trustworthy, only to later stab him in the back. So he just said to Ava, "Well, hopefully he's OK and doesn't get out of control in Vegas."

"Let's work on this prank we keep discussing but never actually do. I would love to pull a marvelous prank on Mr. Awesome. Plus, let's face it, he kinda deserves a reality check anyway," said Mikey.

"Cheeky sprite, Puck," said Wally.

"Wally, are you stroking out on us?" asked Eddie.

"Dude, cheeky sprite Puck is a lute-playing, pointy-eared fairy. Now his vibe was that we should celebrate the devious side of human nature and that few things in life could lift the spirits like a well-played prank."

Eddie's face did its best Biff from *Back to the Future* impersonation. *Cheeky sprite Puck,* his brain said. In response, his face cringed and cowered.

Finally able to speak, Eddie said, "My idea was to put some laxative in his coffee, then remove the toilet paper from the bathroom and only give it to him once he admits to what's going on with people leaving pinball games fucked up."

"That's pretty good, Eddie, but too direct. We want him to volunteer the information," said Mikey. "Once he thinks we know something or are suspicious, we're in trouble."

# HARMLESS

The Piss Rats woke up the next morning at 8:00 a.m. While eating breakfast, they discussed possible pranks to pull on Mr. Awesome. Mikey said, "So here is my idea. We rush into his room in a panicked state, saying there was just breaking news that two people playing pinball caught the Zika virus. That the authorities are positive the pinball machines were spiked with the Zika virus on purpose."

The Rats agreed to Mikey's idea.

Mr. Awesome was still sleeping, so they figured today would be a good time to do it.

Mikey ran into Mr. Awesome's room followed by Eddie and Wally, and he said frantically, "Mr. Awesome, wake up; there's some crazy shit going down."

"Huh, what? What's going on, guys?"

"The media is reporting that the pinball games just gave two people the Zika virus."

Mr. Awesome reached for his glass of water on his bedside stand and said, "Don't worry about that. The Zika virus is harmless.

Everybody gets it in their lifetime. The government just made up the stories about microcephaly. See, boys, every few years, we need to hype up a virus or health scare to secure money for our various agencies, or else those agencies would have to fire people or shut down entirely. With Zika, we all win. Agencies stay open, get funding; they don't have to fire anybody. And then the other companies that manufacture anti-Zika sprays and vaccines and all that garbage make a ton of money as well. So everybody wins with Zika. And don't worry about microcephaly and babies being born with small heads from Zika. It's entirely false. We actually just did a test that had twelve thousand infected women with Zika give birth, and there was zero microcephaly. We already know the next health crisis. It's cockroaches that produce a harmless itchy bite that we, of course, will tell the public could cause you to lose a limb. So, of course, everyone will get their houses sprayed. And like the Zika virus, everybody wins. Exterminators, people making cockroach traps and sprays, vaccines against the cockroaches. Now let Mr. Awesome get a few more hours of shut-eye, *por favor.*"

"But the media wants to shut down the pinball tour because of it!" protested Mikey.

"I will call them after I wake up, and they will cease reporting on this. Then they will come out saying it was a mistake, and pinball is safe." Mr. Awesome then sat up in bed with a grin, slurring his words a little, sounding like Shane MacGowan from the Pogues. "Pinball gets free publicity, so everybody wins again. Mr. Awesome always wins, boys. Always."

The Piss Rats walked back to their rooms, defeated.

"So street drugs in Vegas, yes?" said Eddie. Mikey and Eddie grudgingly agreed.

# BIGFOOT ON A BENDER

J ed and Patti awoke the next morning frazzled and jittery about what today's situation would bring. They measured Jed and compared it to yesterday's results, and they could not believe what they saw. He had grown a quarter inch.

"At this rate, I will be Bigfoot next month!" proclaimed Jed.

"I just don't get it. Should we take you to the ER?" asked Patti.

"I don't know. I mean, just think about it. First, they will assume we're on drugs. Then they will study me like some freak of nature. I am not sure I can handle that. I mean, I try so hard to be uber healthy and avoid this exact situation of having doctors take a stab in the dark on what is needed to fix people. They ultimately conclude that creepy pills with endless side effects are the answer."

"I know, babe, just try to breathe deep and relax."

Jed worked on his breaths. Deep breath in, followed by a slow breath outward. His central nervous system began to relax. Endorphins leaked from every crevice of his brain.

Patti followed suit. They both worked on their breathing, side by side.

"I think I am going to stop taking all my supplements. I mean, it has to be them. I take twenty different pills. I can get my vitamin D from the sun. B vitamins I get from my greens, and omega-3s from chia, walnut, and flaxseed."

"Agreed. Ditch the supplements for sure."

They awoke the next morning and immediately took measurements. Another quarter-inch growth had occurred.

"Dammit," said a panicked Jed. "Screw it. I am done eating healthy as well. Actually, I am done being healthy in general." Jed then surveyed his surroundings to see what debauchery he could inflict upon himself immediately. *A regime of self-destruction must happen ASAP*, he told himself. He saw a rubber band, put it on his wrist, and then stretched it out as far as he could and released it. It came soaring back against his skin. "Ouch."

"What are you doing, Jed?" asked Patti, trying not to grin at her husband's ridiculous attempt at being unhealthy. Jed then smacked his head on the mattress as his wife stood near the doorway with her arms crossed, watching the scene unfold. He then kneeled down and picked up a shoe and began smacking it against his head. Jed kept waiting for his wife to pull the plug on his sudden feral behavior. He would have to do something more extreme to prove to his wife he was serious about this new life decision. He reached for Patti's perfume and began spraying it all over himself.

Finally annoyed, Patti said, "OK, come on, Jed; that's not doing any harm, and now our bedroom just reeks."

Getting angrier and more determined, Jed then considered jumping out the window, but he knew he would surely break something and end up at the one spot he was trying to avoid.

Out of ideas, he screamed, "Something must be causing this! Let's take the kids to IHOP! Then go-karts! Then ice cream! He then walked past Patti and banged his head against the door, producing a mellow dizzy feeling and generating a few bright lights that floated in his horizon.

"Really, IHOP?"

Ignoring her, he walked downstairs, where the vacuum cleaner caught his eye. He turned it on and put the hose to his neck, imagining it was sucking out the poison in his body that was causing his growth. Patti quickly yanked the cord from the electric socket with such force that dull tame sparks burst out. She then looked at her husband. The side effect from his vacuum experiment was a giant hickey, making him look like a teenager or an adult who'd given up on hygiene.

Patti began to reprimand her husband. "Jed, this is ludicrous. Enough of this juvenile, immature behavior. It's not going to solve anything."

"Then what is going to solve this? Because apparently the life I've led, being Mr. Health Nut, has yielded the opposite results I forecasted!"

"Jed, you don't know that; don't draw conclusions."

"I'm sorry. I, well, I just am having a tough time controlling my emotions. I keep picturing myself in a lab being fifteen feet tall with all these wires and tubes sticking out me like a thorn bush."

"I know. I am scared as well."

# CANDY

Their tour bus arrived in Vegas at 1:00 p.m. The Rats looked out the window, expecting shiny bright lights. Instead, they saw a lackluster industrial park that time had forgotten. They saw a dreary sign covered in weeds advertising bingo every Wednesday at 8:00 p.m. They saw some people exit a building and assumed that's where the manufacturing was taking place. The event was scheduled for 7:00 p.m. They had to find drugs fast but had no clue where to begin. They walked down the Strip at a feverish pace, hoping an idea would blossom.

With wide eyes, Eddie commented, "Look at the plethora of strip clubs surrounding us. This is our best option. Plus, we only live once, so a few lap dances would be wise to ease the burden of stress." Eddie felt a pang of guilt rumble inside since Clash was his one and only true love, but him and his band were on a collision course of bending and breaking their morals, so what was one more thing to add to the list?

"I agree with Eddie, man. Strip joints in Vegas seem like the logical choice when you need drugs pretty much now," said Wally, curious about when he had become versed in drugs and strip joints.

"Fine, but business first; once we score the drugs, then you guys can do whatever the hell you want in there," said Mikey.

"So what drugs should we get?" asked Wally nonchalantly, as if he were asking what pizza toppings they should get.

"Ecstasy is ideal. That will get him feeling so gnarly he will feel guilty if he doesn't answer our questions. Cocaine should be easy to get, so it wouldn't hurt to score some of that. No heroin or crack. Actually, mushrooms and acid would work too if we can't find any Ecstasy," said Eddie, proud that his proficiency of street drugs had finally came to fruition.

"OK, sounds good; let's do this shit," said Mikey, embracing his thug side.

They strolled down the street and then paused when they saw a building that advertised "Girls Girls Girls." Instinctively, like it was coded in their DNA, they bought tickets, and it was time to enjoy the ride. Their eyes scanned the room looking for the bar when a dazzling, radiant woman appeared, congenial and undaunted, taking Wally's hand and forcing him to walk with her.

"Hey, sweetie, my name is Candy. You're so adorable, all dressed in black with those matchstick arms, wickedly macabre." She then pseudo-licked his entire body as if it were covered with honey and she was the queen bee who needed a lifetime supply of substance or else she would expire and perish immediately.

Wally instantly began to blush as a fire alarm rang and resonated inside his stomach cavity. Vigorously anti everything, a strip club was a foreign destination. He had been a patron a few times before and always told the strippers politely he was gay, which proved to be a success. But this time, he didn't even have time to say, "Sorry, I'm gay." Her hand was already connected to his leading him through the bright, boisterous strip club. Had he even spoken yet? Isn't something like this a mutual agreement, so each side is satisfied and content? He wasn't feeling content. She pushed him into a private booth.

"Don't worry about money, honey. Once I am done, you will pay any price."

She sat on Wally's lap, and her sizable breasts swung left to right. He felt like a boxer dodging jabs while the commentary called the fight.

"Candy's left breast launches into Wally's face."

"That was an intelligent move by Candy. She knew Wally's defenses were down, so a strike of the breast into his face was wide open. Wally will have to learn to dodge Candy's breasts quicker or this lap dance will be over in the first minute."

After three minutes, Candy climbed off Wally and whispered into his ear, "Come hang out in my private room."

Rational thought seemed to vanish and move like a ghost. He followed his new master, oblivious to everything around him. She opened a door, and they climbed up a set of stairs. Another door opened, and they walked down a hallway with hot-pink walls. At the end of the hallway was a door that said "Candy."

Wally walked in, and the room was full of psychedelic posters. The swirling, bright, trippy colors reminded him of Spencer's Gifts and freshman dorm rooms.

Wally took a seat on the edge of the bed and again asked himself if she had asked him yet if he was OK with this maniac pace of acquaintanceship.

She tossed some condoms on the bed and said, "Don't be nervous, sugar. Just take your clothes off, and I will do the rest."

Finally, Wally spoke. "Yeah, sorry, just very nervous. Do you have any Ecstasy?"

She giggled and said, "Of course I do; it's Vegas." She walked over to a cabinet with a lock on it. *Fuck*, Wally thought. He stood up and tried to watch her unlock it. All he saw were a four and an eight.

She walked back toward him and said, "You're the first cus-tomer who asked for drugs instead of fucking me the second you walked in."

Wally blushed again and said, "Oh, I just want this night to be special, and what better way than taking Ecstasy and fucking you all night."

*What the hell did I just say?* But he knew he would have to play a role here. Over the past decade of his life, whenever he didn't like something, he wouldn't participate in it. It was that simple. He was not used to compromising his values, with a stripper and drugs no less.

Her enormous tits swung back and forth as she smiled at his lie. His plan was to spit out the pill and then try to steal a few more.

That plan came to a screeching halt when she said, "Here, snort this line so you can start rolling immediately. Oh, darling, we're going to have so much fun tonight."

His heart almost beat out of his chest. *How do you fake-snort shit?* Wally had never done Ecstasy before. He always connected it with raves, which he wasn't a huge fan of. However, he never actually had been to a rave before, so it's possible he could have enjoyed them. He was a huge music fan, so he listened to electronic music here and there, but raves and that scene just weren't him, he as-sumed. His mind raced. He needed a plan in the next thirty sec-onds. The palms of his hands were saturated with sweat. He had nothing. There was nothing he could do.

Candy went first. She bent over and said, "Oh baby, can you hold my hair while I do this?"

Wally walked over to the naked stripper and held her hair while she snorted a two-inch-long line of Ecstasy. She dropped the dollar bill, tilted her head back, held her nose, and snorted like a teen-ager with a cold. She swallowed and made a sour face. "It always tastes so gross," she said with a chuckle.

Wally's turn was next. His only plan was to accidentally sneeze on the Ecstasy. But with Candy being right next to him, already touching him and looking like she was in heaven, would he really be able to make it look like an accident? And wouldn't she just get more if he accidently sneezed on it?

*Fuck*, he thought, *I can't ruin this. It's probably the only joy in this poor stripper's life.* So he grabbed the rolled-up dollar bill and snorted. He had never snorted anything before. He thought to himself, *That wasn't bad.* Then a minute later, he snorted again as liquids started dripping from his nose, and it hit him. He coughed and felt the Ecstasy hit his taste buds. It tasted like a sewer. Candy was kissing his neck for what seemed like an eternity. *Is it already working?* he thought. *Why am I letting a stripper give me a hickey? Why are my legs feeling so tingly? Is my heart still beating? Where am I?* Then it began. The Ecstasy worked its way to his brain, and he was paralyzed with bliss. He lay down in the bed with Candy, and they just lay arm in arm, listening to the techno Candy had put on the stereo and staring at all the black light posters.

*First Wally joins forces with the president and then smokes weed, and now he's taking E with a stripper?*

After thirty minutes of the punk and stripper not talking or moving, Candy removed her arms from Wally, kissed him on the cheek, and said, "Let's do some more." Wally didn't move. His eyes were closed, and his body was not going to fight anything. He would do anything she said at this point. He was her slave. Ecstasy was his master.

When he heard a sound, he realized it was his cell phone beeping. Wally tried ignoring it, but like a man of the law delivering a subpoena, it would not quit. He managed to move to the edge of the bed to grab his jeans. He reached inside them, and it was

Mikey. "Any luck?" That message shook him out of his Ecstasy-induced coma.

He walked over to Candy, who was unlocking her vault, and grabbed her and spun her around so she was facing him. He began fondling her breasts and then began to kiss and lick each one. She moaned in pleasure. He said, "Baby, just leave some pills out so we can get them at our own leisure."

She smiled, grabbed his crotch, and said, "Sure." She handed him a pill and said, "Chew this one up." An internal battle raged in his mind. This time he could fake it. *She's too fucked up to notice if I'm actually chewing it and swallowing.* But his willpower was gone. It was like it never existed to begin with. He told himself, *Just one more pill, and then I'm done.* He picked up the white pill that had 007 stamped on it and began chewing it up. It was the worst thing his mouth had ever tasted. He gagged a few times but managed to swallow and keep it down. The first Ecstasy pill he snorted was finally letting go of its tight grip a bit, but he knew this entire pill would render him powerless. He would be paralyzed in bed with the big-breasted, tattooed stripper for hours, listening to music and feeling like they were inside a cartoon play land. So he'd better think about what needed to be done now while the first line of Ecstasy slowly wore off.

First, he had to steal some pills. But when? He couldn't now; that would be too obvious. In a few hours, he would steal some.

Next, text the Rats an update. He responded to Mikey's text with "In a room with a stripper, should be able to get some E, but it's gonna take a few hours."

He felt lips on his neck, and Candy was feeling frisky. They lay in bed naked, holding each other, while the pills they'd just chewed up took complete control of their minds, bodies, and souls. They both closed their eyes for the first thirty minutes and then began to say things like, "I feel so good," "This is amazing," and "I am so fucked up right now."

After the second hour, the Ecstasy began to allow them to move and talk. Candy got up and went to the bathroom. *Now is the time*, thought Wally. He walked over to the cabinet where the pile of E was. He took three pills, returned to the bed, and put them in his wallet. Candy walked out just as he came back to bed. She began kissing him and touching his crotch. Wally was not about to have sex with a stripper. He thought of his only excuse. He told Candy he was actually gay.

She said, "Well, even gay guys enjoy this."

Three hours later, Wally left Candy's room with three pills and $3,000 less in his bank account. As he was walking down the hallway, he thought to himself, *There must have been an easier way to figure out if Mr. Awesome is hiding something*. Then he thought about returning to the room with Candy and eating E with her the rest of his life.

He walked down the flight of stairs and back to the main room where all the stripper poles were. He craved a tall, cold glass of water. Again, before he could even get a drink, the hottest woman approached him and went to take his hand, but this time he hastily removed it and said, "Sorry, I'm gay."

He ordered his water.

He texted Mikey: "Where you at?"

"We're at the bar on the corner of this street. Just look for a yellow flashing sign that says ' Vegas #1 Bar.'"

Wally took three long sips from his water and dumped the rest on his face, licking at the sides of his lips to try to get some of the falling water into his dehydrated system. He remembered hearing that staying hydrated on Ecstasy was critical. He wished he hadn't poured most of his water on his face like some feral subhuman creature just released from a cage who had never used a glass before.

Walking down the street, everything now seemed different. The buildings had a strange tint to them. The sidewalk looked like it was moving with him. He tried to shake it all off and keep his mind straight. He went into the bar, looked around, and saw Mikey and Eddie standing near the pool table.

"Hey," said Wally.

"Fuck, Wally, what took so long? It's almost seven," said Mikey.

"Whatever, man. I got three pills of Ecstasy, so piss off."

"Just three?" questioned Eddie. "Wally, we're in Vegas, and we're basically rich." He looked around and then pulled out a handful of miscellaneous drugs.

Wally thought to himself, *Maybe I should have taken a few more.*

They returned to the bus, and the Rats put their newly acquired drugs on the table. Various shapes and designs. Bright purple with stars on them. Orange triangles. Square tabs. Powder that looked like it had been scooped off the ground after a recent snowstorm.

"So," said Eddie, "we have plenty of Ecstasy. I am thinking we crush a pill up and dose his water or soda or whatever the hell he's drinking. If that doesn't do the trick, well, shit, we have more Ecstasy. And we can always give him some acid. That's the last resort though, as acid could totally cause a mental overload. Then the cocaine, Valium, and weed I will just keep as reserves." Eddie had other plans for those drugs. Mainly personal consumption.

# THERE WILL BE NO BOILING BONES ON THIS PROPERTY

The Rats were on autopilot during the event. Their minds were focused on later that night.

Mikey's mind wondered how this would all work out. Wouldn't Mr. Awesome know if he was super high? Surely he would know that he had been given something.

After the event, Mikey told Eddie and Wally to ditch the plan of spiking Mr. Awesome's drink.

"So, what, you're making all the decisions now, Mikey?" questioned Eddie.

"Eddie, it doesn't make sense. Spiking Mr. Awesome's drink is too dangerous. He will know it was spiked. He won't trust us. We will get fired. We won't get paid. Let's just convince him that it's Vegas, and we should party hard and celebrate," said Wally.

"OK, calm down, spazz," said Eddie.

Was Wally yelling or screaming, or was Eddie just being Eddie? He couldn't tell at this point.

"Another successful night," said Mr. Awesome as he got on the bus and began walking to his room. The Rats looked at one another and knew they had to say something instantly.

Eddie spoke up. "Hey, Mr. Awesome, how about we all celebrate tonight? We've been having so much success, and 'What happens in Vegas, stays in Vegas.'"

Mr. Awesome stared at Eddie for a full minute without blinking or saying anything. "Yes, let's celebrate. We all deserve to let loose and enjoy the fruits of our labor."

The Rats started feeling less guilty about their previous plan of spiking the drink of the president of the United States with Ecstasy. Now, they told themselves, it was going to be a fun night out, and if the president took some pills they gave him, well, at least it wouldn't be forced upon him.

*Who the hell cares? Spike it with one thousand tabs of acid. This guy is the enemy of punks, dammit!*

They all cracked beers on the bus, and the tension among everybody was visible miles away. Nobody really said much.

Mr. Awesome finally spoke, "So, boys, let's not spend our one night in Vegas hanging out on the bus. Let's hit the Strip."

Eddie took all the drugs from today's score with him like a dog with a new bone. He absolutely loved taking drugs and even loved all the other facets involved. The act of scoring the drug and dealing with shady individuals who at any moment could snap and try to cause a rupture in your organs. The anticipation of doing the drug and waiting for it to take hold. Then, of course, the drug itself and how great he felt on it. Even coming down he enjoyed, as it gave him a new perspective on things.

He resisted the urge to take a few Valiums or a hit of some weed. Usually, he wouldn't walk around with this amount of drugs on him, but he assumed since he was with the president, he had immunity from the law.

*I have seen Eddie many times choose drugs over a woman until he met Clash.*

They went into the first bar they saw. Mikey asked Ava what she wanted to drink. She said Coors Light was fine. Mikey ordered two Coors Lights and then a shot of whiskey for himself. Eddie and Wally were already laughing with Mr. Awesome as they downed double shots and pounded half a Bud Light.

"Here you go," said Mikey, handing Ava her beer.

"I saw you take that shot of whiskey. Why do you need to be drunk to hang out with me?"

Mikey felt a little guilty and then told her Coors Lights didn't really do anything for him; his body didn't believe it was beer, but instead spoiled orange juice, so it didn't give him a buzz. She laughed and punched him softly in the arm.

*I would be doing shots all the time if I had to hang out with the president and the president's assistant.*

"So, Mr. Awesome, what's up with aliens, man? I mean, come on, we're your crew now—shed some light, bro," said Eddie.

Mr. Awesome smiled, adjusted his glasses, and said, "Edward, aliens are as real as you want them to be."

"Bullshit response. Dude, I don't have a tape recorder or anything; just tell me, man."

"Fine. They exist."

"Why such secrecy, then?"

"Because we don't have the technology to reach out to them yet. But they have the technology to reach us. So imagine if the public knew that aliens could appear at any time on earth. It would cause mass hysteria. So when they do decide to investigate earth and happen to be seen or killed, it's our top priority to cover it up."

"So like Roswell, New Mexico, or whatever, is a legit alien cover-up?

"Again, aliens are as real as you want them to be."

"Ha-ha-ha. OK, I think I feel your vibe. I am going to go tell some random strangers now."

Mr. Awesome's boozy brain questioned how much he could trust the misfit.

*Maybe I am an alien, and I will go back to my planet soon.*

They left after an hour and went to a huge bar with luminous lights and waitresses dressed in tight shirts. Like clockwork, beer and shots appeared in front of them. Mikey's brain began to feel the effects of the booze. He looked at Ava and tried to give her a sly, confident grin, and then he looked around the bar. In each corner were Secret Service agents trying to blend in but failing miserably.

"So, Mr. Awesome, since it's Vegas, ya feel like cranking the party to the next level?" said Eddie.

He laughed and said, "Edward, you do realize I am the president, and you're asking the president to commit a felony with some punks."

"Well, what if I told you I scored some Ecstasy earlier today—would you be interested?"

Mr. Awesome laughed a little again, took a sip of his beer, looked around the bar, and then tried acting durable and brawny as the sentence "I'd be down for the cause" slid out his mouth.

Eddie gave him the pill and then said, "Hey, you two, come here." Mikey and Ava walked over, and Eddie said, "Listen, it's Vegas and our only night here. Mr. Awesome is going to take some E with us. You down?"

Mikey looked at Ava, and Ava said, "Yeah, I don't know; I think I might sit this one out."

Mikey tried not to look disappointed and casually said, "More for us, then."

Eddie handed everybody except Ava a pill. He suggested they chew half of it first to test the potency, since pills on the market these days were very strong. They tried acting casual and not making too much of a scene. But if anybody looked at their group in that thirty seconds, they would have seen a group of adults twisting and turning their facial muscles as if they just drank motor oil instead of a stout.

While waiting for the pills to find the brain's serotonin and unleash a grandiose amount of it, Mr. Awesome asked Mikey to explain more about how his dad brought back pinball in 1976.

"Well, in the early forties, pinball was seen as a form of gambling, so it was banned in most major cities. The popular phrase was—well, if you're hip to pinball, it's popular—'Pinball is a game of chance, not skill.' Thus, it was a type of gambling."

"This wasn't some lighthearted ban, either; they really were serious. In the seventies, New York's mayor would take sledgehammers and smash pinball machines while tossing the remnants into the river. His particular beef was that it robbed kids of precious hard-earned nickels and dimes. So my dad in 1976 testified to a committee in a Manhattan courtroom that pinball was not a game of chance but skill. Inside the courtroom, there were a few pinball machines, for him to prove his statement. He would call out his shots, indicating that it was not a game of chance, but actually of skill. The committee was so impressed that they lifted in the ban in New York, and other cities followed suit. However, in Kokomo, Indiana, they just lifted the ordinance banning pinball in 2006 and in Ocean City, New Jersey, your not supposed to play Pinball on Sundays.

"Well, then, let's make sure there is not a rally scheduled for Ocean City on a Sunday then," said Mr. Awesome letting out a hardy laugh. Nobody else found it amusing since there was no need to reiterate the obvious.

"Actually, fuck that. Let's purposely have a rally there on Sunday. America needs to know that Pinball is badass and nothing can be done to slow it down, especially pointless rules like not playing on Sundays. Eddie then searched online for other dumb rules in NJ they could violate. He read out loud to everybody.

*It is against the law to "frown" at a police officer.*
*It is illegal to get drunk and annoy others in your house.*
*You may not slurp your soup.*
*It is illegal to throw ashes on the sidewalk.*
*All cats must wear three bells to warn birds of their whereabouts.*
*Cross-dressing is illegal.*
*It is forbidden for a woman, on a Sunday, to walk down Broad Street without wearing a petticoat.*
*Pickles are not to be consumed on Sundays and not to be thrown on the sidewalk.*
*There will be no boiling of bones on the property.*
*No one may annoy someone of the opposite sex.*
*It is illegal to purchase ice cream after 6 p.m. without a doctor's note.*

"So Mr. Awesome, I finally understand why your so stressed! You must not be able to sleep trying to make sure all cats have three bells and no pickles are consumed on Sundays!" said Eddie.

"I just texted the VP to look into this nonsense," said Mr. Awesome slightly embarrassed.

Eddie's mind went bonkers thinking about how much fun it would be violating all these rules in a single day; adding to his already large collection of broken rules him and the Piss Rats were collecting.

They left the bar and began walking down the street. Mr. Awesome saw a strip club and walked in without saying anything to the Rats or Ava. A woman approached Mr. Awesome, and he smacked her ass. She looked surprised, as she was usually the instigator, not the customer. Mr. Awesome disappeared after just one minute in the strip club.

Wally couldn't believe it when Candy approached him. "So the gay guy is back in the all-naked female strip club."

Wally tried not looking too uncomfortable and said half-jokingly, "Want to go back to your room and take more E?"

She didn't smile or show any emotions this time. It was all business: $3,000 for the night. *Fuck*, Wally thought. Was he a punk or just another rich businessman on the Strip, blowing thousands on strippers and drugs? He knew the earlier drugs were amazing, but $3,000 was a lot of money, even if Mr. Awesome was paying them $100,000 each.

Candy interrupted his daydreaming. "So what's it going to be? I have other customers who will easily pay that. I mean, look at me." Wally looked at her skinny body covered with tattoos and big tits and said, "Three thousand dollars it is yet again."

*So $6,000 total now that Mr. Anti-Everything Punk Rocker has blown on strippers and drugs. If I am an alien, I request my visit to Earth be finished and to please beam me back to my normal planet.*

Eddie's plan was to have lap dances with every stripper. But he would need to do something he wasn't exactly great at. Practicing the art of restraint. Not get so sloshed that he spent all his time with the strippers and abandoned the real task at hand, which was the interrogation of the president.

After many hours, Mr. Awesome came back to the main floor looking somewhat sober. *Fuck*, thought Eddie who'd just finished his seventeenth lap dance and was trying to rank the top three so he could schedule them again. *The Ecstasy must have worn off. I am going to give him another pill and then suggest he take this other pill as well. Which will be LSD. But I won't mention the actual name of it.*

"Hey, Mr. Awesome, have fun upstairs?" said Eddie.

"Edward, I love being the leader of the free world!"

"So, Mr. Awesome, we all nibbled on some more pills, so it's your turn to take more, OK?"

"Edward, I love this Ecstasy; give me more."

His right arm extended outward and his palm faced upward. Then surprisingly, his left hand joined him and made a cup with both hands as if he were about to receive Holy Communion from a priest. Eddie dropped the Ecstasy and LSD into the makeshift religious symbol and tried not to think about it being a bomb and exploding, causing mass injuries and time spent behind iron bars.

"Child, you have come here today to bear witness to the reincarnation of God's son, Jesus. Swallow this square tab and chew this pill, and show Jesus you love and worship him."

Mr. Awesome asked what the square tab was, and Eddie said, "Oh, I don't know, but we all took it, and we're feeling tremendous. Like total superstars." Mr. Awesome nodded and said he trusted his boys and, without hesitation, popped it into his mouth.

Mr. Awesome suggested they rent an entire floor of a hotel to commit endless sins.

Eddie couldn't believe how smooth this was going. No turbulence so far. Eddie texted Wally: "Gave Awesome LSD. He's renting an entire floor of a hotel. Will text you the address. Hope you're having fun, and be safe."

As they were leaving, Mr. Awesome offered a stripper $5,000 to come to the hotel with them. Mikey and Ava couldn't believe the carelessness of Mr. Awesome, not to mention the fact that he was married. Mikey tried removing the guilty state of mind taking shape inside him and the thoughts running through his mind that he could be affecting the president's marriage just to pry and pull information about what was really going on with those pinball machines. *If* there was anything rotten happening at all. This was all starting to spread like a wildfire. He tried to rationalize it all. People were fine before pinball and then were not fine after pinball. Johnny was missing. Mr. Awesome has been acting very weird lately. This was enough of a reason to commit many felonies, right? He still wasn't sure. But they were in too deep now. No turning back. Steadfast with conviction and grit.

Mr. Awesome, the stripper, Eddie, Mikey, and Ava took the elevator to their new zip code, the thirteenth floor. Mr. Awesome told his security guards to stand at each end of the floor and not to let anybody in or out.

Eddie wished that Mr. Awesome didn't cough up $5,000 for the stripper. Not only was he married, but this was going to make the entire process more cumbersome.

Eddie texted Mikey: "Dude, this going to be tough. We need to get that stripper away from him and we need to do something about Ava."

Mikey responded: "Don't worry. Once the acid kicks in, he won't give a shit about her. Then we'll begin drilling him for oil."

"Eddie, our lovely female friend here is asking what drugs you have available."

Eddie thought, *Maybe if I put them all on the table, it will occupy her while I rap to Mr. Awesome.* Eddie reached into his pocket and grabbed a handful of pills and powders and baggies and put them on the table. Then he tried to spread them out so the stripper would have a tough time deciphering what was what. A cacophony of sorts.

"So, Mr. Awesome, how you feeling?" asked Eddie. There was a knock on the door, and Eddie thought, *God fuckin' dammit, can't I just try to speak to the president alone for one fucking minute without being interrupted?*

Mikey walked over to the door and looked through the peep-hole. It was Wally. Mikey opened the door and said, "Hey, Wally, how you doing?"

Wally tried to act like he was fine. "Yeah, man, I am cool." But he was a bit shaken over everything. Just a few weeks ago, he had been living righteously. His way. Zero compromises. Now all he did was compromise.

"Can you do me a huge favor," said Mikey to Ava. "The Rats need to talk to Mr. Awesome for fifteen minutes. Can you talk to the stripper or just keep her away?"

Ava agreed, and Mikey breathed a sigh of relief. He was not in the mood to persuade Ava to give them some time with Mr. Awesome and then also explain to her why they needed this time.

Eddie began talking first while the other Piss Rats surrounded Mr. Awesome. "So, Mr. Awesome, we have been noticing people leaving, but before he could complete his sentence, like a ferret let out of a cage, the stripper bolted past Ava, yelling and laughing. "Let's get fucked up!" She started handing out pills and powders and joints. She was like a drill sergeant. If you didn't take what she gave you, it was a lap dance and down the gullet.

Twelve hours later, Eddie opened his eyes and surveyed his sur-roundings. *Looked to be a hotel room*, he thought. He went to move and felt pain spread through every cell in his body. Finally in an upward position, and eager to remedy his pain, he began the jour-ney of trying to piece together last night when it was interrupt-ed by noticing the door to the hotel room had been blown off. Walking over to inspect it, he caught his reflection in a mirror and he was dressed like a ninja. *What the fuck happened last night.* He then looked around the room and there were throwing stars stuck in all the walls. He ran out of the room into the hallway try-ing to maintain his mental state. He had been on the wrong side of many morning blackouts, but this one might rank as number one. As he walked down the hallway, every door had been blown of the hinges leaving remnants of burnt wood splattered all over the place. He peered in a random room and there was a huge hole in the wall that was caused by a grenade or rocket launcher. Another door had a axe stuck in it. Finally he found Mr. Awesome's room. He walked in and the room resembled a weapons convention. He picked up a dagger knife off the bed that looked like it belonged in Scotland not L.A. There were nunchucks, brass knuckles that doubled as knives and even a black cat key chain that was also used for mace, a knife and even a vaporizer. In the corner of the room he noticed a rocket launcher. Walking over to take a closer look he saw weapons galore; semi automatic rifles, machines guns, grenades, revolvers and a mortar.

Instantly his mind has a seizure wondering if he killed Mr. Awesome last night. Frantically he searches for him. Finally Eddie spots Mr. Awesome passed out on the patio. Eddie kicks him lightly praying for movement. A raised arm signals survival. "Help me up." Eddie lifts him and then lets go, causing Mr. Awesome to fall right back down. If he wasn't dead before, he probably was now concluded Eddie. He ran out of the room and down the hall of destruction. There was shattered sharp glass from broken bottles and windows everywhere. French fries and pizza mixed in with empty bullet chasings. He went to press the elevator button, but fearing that was also blown up, he took the stairs.

The Rats regrouped in the lobby. "I fucking pray somebody got some info from Mr. Asshole last night," said Mikey.

Wally and Eddie had guilty looks on their faces. Both had succumbed to the drugs and partying, forgetting their mission.

"Fuck, fuck, fuck," said Mikey.

The Rats were in a daze from the night before and in shock that they hadn't accomplished and succeeded in their assignment.

Wally had left early, so exhausted from his $6,000 dollars spent on strippers and Ecstasy while Mikey convinced the security guards to release him so he could hang with Ava instead, leaving Eddie alone to party with the president and the stripper.

"What about the stripper Mr. Awesome was with? Maybe she got some shit?" said Eddie delicately enough as to not cause more tension and swelling of his brain.

"Shit, yeah, let's go try to find her," said Mikey.

They left the hotel and went back to the strip club.

"Let's make this quick. I am starving and ready to puke," said Wally wondering when the last time food had entered his mouth.

They walked into the strip club, and Wally could not believe his eyes as Candy greeted them. "For somebody who is gay, you sure do like strip clubs," she said.

"What the fuck, Wally? You're gay?" said Eddie.

"Yeah, you didn't know your drummer is gay?" said Candy.

"Wait, how does Candy know you're gay? Never mind. Listen, do you know where…shit, I don't even know her name," said Eddie.

"Candy, there was a stripper last night who left with us. Any idea where we can find her? We just want five minutes of her time," said Wally.

"Oh sure, I know her. She's due in tonight."

"Candy, we don't have time to wait that long. We have to leave soon. Can you give us her number?" asked Wally.

"Well, that depends, Gay Wally. I think you're going to have to do whatever I want."

"Yeah, sure, fine, whatever. Make it quick; I am ready to puke."

An hour later, Wally returned sore, bruised, and battered from their S&M session. Ready to collapse, he handed Mikey the phone number and address of the stripper.

They called her, and she agreed to meet up.

"So, listen, we're really sorry about last night. It's just that, well, last night we drugged up the president of the United States. Before you judge us, let me briefly explain. We have every reason to believe the security and safety of all Americans are in peril from a rascal swindler of a president. If you choose to help us, you will go down in history as one of very few courageous and tenacity-laden humans who've risked their lives to save countless others." Eddie felt like he was in a James Bond movie or was an FBI agent trying to save the world. He continued: "The plan was to get audio of him confessing, but, if I may be so blunt, we fucked up. We blacked out, and retrieval of sensitive information was a negative. I know it's a long shot, but any chance Mr. Awesome disclosed anything?"

"Today's your lucky day. Sit down, boys. First of all, the president was totally out of his mind smashed last night. She then pointed at Eddie and said, **"y**ou encouraged that poor man to party way to hard." Eddie felt like a dog receiving discipline from his owner. He responded with, **"y**ou weren't exactly a saint yourself, you know?"

Flashbacks violently entered Eddie's mind. He remembered Mr. Awesome being convinced that he was in severe danger from an invasion of bugs with creepy faces; skull mimic spiders, goofy cross-eyed wasps, devil flower mantises and clown crab spiders. He had seen them on the Science Channel. Then he ordered his security guards to find a twenty four hour weapons store to destroy them all. When his security returned, he was then convinced they were Venezuelan poodle moths and began launching his throwing stars causing them to leave. *Maybe I gave him to much LSD*, thinks Eddie.

The stripper continued. So yeah, acid, Ecstasy, weed, wine, cocaine, nitrous balloons. A copious intake. As if the word 'overdose' was never, ever in his lexicon. A majority of the time, he spoke gibberish; it made no sense at all. A babbling fool who begged and pleaded about nothing at all. Then all of a sudden, all the chemicals and poisons pulsating in and out of every cell must have aligned perfectly, producing a coherent and civilized tone. He spoke about what was digging into his soul, and that is what you fear the most, guys.

"Big pharma offered him twenty million dollars for carte blanche. Complete immunity. Charlatans with nothing to fear.

Their first act of malfeasance was the timeless act of transformation from human to animal. Theater and literature have explored this countless times in such classics as *The Fly, American Werewolf in London,* and *The Island of Dr. Moreau.*"

As if jolted by ten thousand bolts of electricity and engulfed in a full bodysuit of barbed wire, the Rats finally figured out what happened to Johnny and it was something their brains never had imagined.

"Then they wanted to test new pills by releasing the medications via the buttons on pinball machines. Apparently he was looking for ways to allow Big Pharma to test these new experimental meds and once he received Mikey's email about Pinball Manfacturing, he contacted Big Pharma and told them about it and they decided to move forward with their evil plan. He told me he felt so guilty about it that he started self-medicating himself by playing pinball without gloves on so the meds would absorb into him, providing a mental vacation."

"So the president turned our singer into an animal, then? And where the hell was I during this confession?" asked Eddie.

Wally screamed and then puked again.

"Ignoring Eddie she said, "Your singer is now a rat. I am so sorry."

"I am going to fucking kill him," shouted Eddie.

Cleaning the vomit from his lips, Wally said, "So I guess this solves the creepy midnight procedure to inject metal into our hands. He didn't want us to absorb the test pharmaceuticals."

"Yeah, I suspect that's the main reason why. OK, we need a game plan," said Mikey.

The Rats thanked the stripper and went back to their hotel. They were too hungover to make any rash decisions, so they decided to ponder things and decide on a course of action upon awakening from slumber.

# RUBY A-GO-GO

Luckily they had an off day today. It was as if the person scheduling the tour saw Vegas and assumed there would be cognitive problems and bodies feeling like dumpsters the following day.

The next morning, Mr. Awesome ate breakfast with the Rats and Ava. The Rats tried their hardest to pretend everything was normal. They asked the president about the upcoming rally.

"Well, boys, it's going to be held in LA. You're going to dress up as workers from the docks."

They all nodded and tried to express interest. After the president and Ava left, the Rats discussed how they were going to deal with Mr. Awesome.

"I have an idea," said Wally. "What if we have another night like in Vegas, and I have Candy or her friend tape-record him admitting what he did."

"A brief side note, Wally. What's up with you and her? She said you're gay?" said Eddie.

"It's a long story and quite fucked up," said Wally. "But rest assured, I am not gay, and what I did was for Johnny. Plus, what would it matter if I were gay? Anyway, is this a good idea, or are we just digging ourselves an even bigger chasm? I feel like we might be."

"Wally, it would only matter because you were not honest with us, and that's not cool. You know the first rule of this band is honesty," said Eddie.

"Guys, come on; focus on the issue at hand. And Eddie, I highly doubt you're honest with us one hundred percent of the time. I think it's absolutely necessary to have something on audio. I mean, if we don't have anything concrete, it's our word against the US government. Not only do we lose, but most likely we melt away like butter in the summer sun. We need audio or something written. He obviously is not going to write anything down. So that leaves audio," said Mikey.

"Fuck, let's just do it," said a defeated Eddie.

"Yeah, is Candy there?" said Wally.

"She's working," said the bartender.

"Can I have her cell number?"

"We don't do that."

"Can you just tell her it's Gay Wally?"

"Ooohhh, Gay Wally. Yeah, we heard about you. Let me get the number."

Wally hung up the phone, and told the Rats' the good news. "OK, got her number. But she's working. Her break is at two p.m., and we will call her then."

The Piss Rats returned to their beds to rest their weary, achy bones while also praying that their brains would stop replaying every single scenario over and over, including the ones where they could go to jail for a voluminous length of time.

"Hey, guys, it's about that time to throw our Hail Mary pass and see if Candy can catch it in the end zone," said Wally.

"Man, I was just in the middle of a dream where I was in a band with Johnny Peebucks from the Swingin' Utters and Nick Blinko from Rudimentary Peni, and we were playing a secret show on

Jupiter. Clash was there, and we had a baby with guitars instead of arms, and so then I picked up my baby and began playing his guitar arms, and you caused this dream to cease, Wally. I hope you're just thrilled at your shitty accomplishment."

Wally momentarily thought about spray-painting "asshole" on Eddie's forehead when a breeze from the open window brought him back to the task at hand.

"Hey, Candy, it's Wally."

"Hiya, Gay Wally. I heard you might be calling today. What's up?"

"In the future or even right now, Wally is fine. So without diving into a pool of rusty nails and grimy knives by explaining what I am going to request next, can you ask that stripper if she's interested in an easy five thousand dollars? We're willing to pay her five thousand dollars if she repeats the night she had in Vegas with Mr. Awesome, *but* she needs to record it all and have him confess. No recorded confession, and we only pay her for her time. Also, have her download a free voice recorder app as well since this is pretty much our lives on the line and we can't risk crappy foreign made gadgets not working correctly.

"Seems like tape-recording the president of the United States and possibly ruining his life is worth a little more money than that, Wallard."

"It's Wally. Fine, eight thousand dollars, and one thousand dollars for you convincing her."

"Make it ten thousand dollars and two thousand dollars for me just giving her this message. I am not convincing her. In fact, I want nothing at all to do with your hush-hush unsavory bullshit."

"Yeah, that's fine. Thanks, Candy."

"No problem, Wall Wall. I will let you know."

"Candy is going to ask the stripper," said Wally as he hung up.

"Does this stripper have a name besides 'stripper'? Also, does Candy like ever not work, jeez, she must have insane stamina," commented Mikey.

"Oh yeah, sorry. Her name is Ruby A-Go-Go and yeah Candy is quite the lady, holy shit," said Wally.

"What a charismatic and provocative name. If I were a stripper and a female, I could see myself being a Ruby A-Go-Go," said Eddie.

The Rats felt sleazy and vile from the astounding amount of partying they'd been doing and from digesting the news that Mr. Awesome most likely turned their singer into a rat. Then there was the releasing of test pharmaceuticals via pinball machines and the $300,000 he'd paid them, which obviously was nothing at all to him since Big Pharma paid him $20 million. They wondered how they got into this mess? How they got into punk rock? Why couldn't they just have gone to college, wrangled a job, and procured a wife and kids like countless others who appeared bloated and satisfied with their lives? How much more could they handle? They felt like rats in a race. The one thing in life they'd tried avoiding was now their reality.

Wally's phone ringing shook everybody from their reveries.

"Hey, Candy."

"So, Wall, Ruby accepted your proposition."

Wally gave the other two Rats a thumbs-up and attempted a slight smile, producing a dollop of dopamine.

"Thanks, Candy. I really appreciate you helping us. So we would want Ruby to take a flight out to LA ASAP. We will pay for the flight, obviously. Also, can we give your money to Ruby? Or do you want a money transfer or something?"

"You can give the money to her, and I hope you guys find what you're looking for, Willie Wall. See ya soon."

Wally thought to himself, *I really hope I don't see you soon. And what does that exactly mean? Fuck it.*

"Later, Candy. Thanks again."

# THE DYING ELK HERD

The LA rally went smoothly. Around 8:00 p.m., they all met up on the bus.

"Another successful rally, Mr. Awesome. Well done," said Wally.

"Rats we are visionaries. Modern-day Columbuses."

"Mikey's the visionary, and Columbus wiped out an entire race of humans, so perhaps you're a tad astray with your words," said Eddie.

"So how about we go get a few beers and explore LA," said Mikey.

"Rats, have you noticed that we seem to constantly celebrate with drugs and alcohol? I mean, can't we all just agree that Mikey's idea along with my awe-inspiring spine-tingling authority has been a success and just get a good night's rest? I was looking up alcoholism, and I am pretty sure we're the poster boys for it."

"I agree, Mr. Awesome. So let's just go have a beer or two or three, and you will feel better about your booze problem, since beer makes you feel better and helps you forget about your problems," said Eddie.

Mr. Awesome thought about this statement by Eddie. As illogical and backward as it was, goddamn if it weren't true. A few beers would make him feel better about his recent alcohol problems.

They hit up the closest bar and began *"Operation Annihilation Intoxication Inebriation."*

"Shots, shots, shots," the Rats chanted.

A few hours later, everyone was wasted except Wally. He needed to be somewhat coherent to orchestrate the plan.

Wally would suggest they hit up another bar, and then as they were walking, he would steer everybody into a predetermined strip club. Ruby A-Go-Go would tell Mr. Awesome the Rats bought him a free lap dance, and then Ruby would convince Mr. Awesome they should go party at her place again. Ruby had already talked to the owner of the strip club about using one of their booths for a lap dance. In exchange, Ruby would mention his strip club to her friends as being a phenomenal place to dance.

As they were walking down the street, Eddie realized this would be one of the last times they'd be able to try to manipulate Mr. Awesome into leaking some top-secret information.

"So, Mr. Awesome, all day people have their claws out fighting one another to earn a income, but in the end, isn't it all worthless unless we rise up and destroy the impending robot invasion? I mean, ninety-five million have no jobs now, and robots and automation are just going to steal more and more jobs. So aren't we doomed until we address this issue?"

"Eddie, I always knew your brain was constantly churning and chugging."

Eddie waited for Mr. Awesome to say more, but that was it. *The most important issue of our time, and that's all I get?*

"Dude, that's it? You're not going to do anything else to fix this? Then why even bother doing this pinball crap if, in the end, it's all void from robots?"

"Eddie, trust me, I share your concern, but what can I do? Unless the masses revolt and protest against automation ruining society, my hands are tied."

"So humanity is basically a dying elk herd?" said Eddie.

He wanted to say more, but they were approaching the strip club, and it was time for serious business.

# BIG PHARMA

After Mr. Awesome left with Ruby inside the strip club, the Rats then had to fight off the strippers. If it were like Vegas, this would have been impossible. They politely refused many times, and luckily, fifteen minutes later, a drunken, grinning Mr. Awesome walked over to the Rats with Ruby and said, "Hey, boys, I'm gonna go party with Rudy at her place. Wanna join?"

"We are good," Mikey said. "You go have fun—you earned it. We're gonna go have a few more drinks and see you tomorrow."

"You sure, boys? Ruby has a pool and Jacuzzi and probably some friends, wink, wink."

"We're good," Mikey said again. "Go enjoy yourself."

"This better work," said an increasingly annoyed Eddie. "I want that asshole to pay for what he did to Johnny."

"Shit, did anybody give Ruby some drugs that she could use on Mr. Awesome?" asked Mikey.

"We're all set. I gave her seven pills of E, one hit of acid, some blow, and weed."

"What about nitrous balloons? Apparently, the president of the United States loves nitrous," said Mikey.

"That's a negative on the nitrous, guys," said Eddie.

"So what's the plan for the rest of the evening? I've only had a few drinks. Actually, I just remembered, Blazing Eye is playing in LA tonight." said Wally.

"Lets just call it a night. Blazing Eye is playing with Exit Order at the Church in Philly in September, maybe we can catch them then," said Mikey

They woke up the next morning, and their curiosity about Ruby and Mr. Awesome was overwhelming. Eddie woke up first at 9:00 a.m. and immediately woke up Wally and Mikey. "Dude, guys, wake up. I am dying to know what happened last night."

Wally grabbed his cell phone, and there was one new message. His heart rate increased. "Guys, I have a new message!"

"Fuckin' read it!" shouted Eddie.

"Success. Call me after eleven a.m."

They all smiled.

"Well, it sucks that we have to wait a few hours, but it sounds like we owe her a ton of cash," said Wally.

"Yup, it's fine. I would pay almost any price to get this information on tape," said Eddie.

They called Ruby at 11:03 a.m.

"Hello."

"Hey, Ruby, it's Wally."

"Oh, hey, Wally. So we were successful last night. I gave him two pills of E, a hit of acid, and a bunch of weed. He's still sleeping. When he wakes up, I will drop him off along with the tape, and you can pay me."

"Great, thanks so much, Ruby. Hey, can you do us one last favor? Can you play over the phone the part of him confessing?"

"Let's just wait until I drop the tape off, OK?"

"Yeah, sure, that's fine. Thanks again."

"She's going to drop him off when he wakes up, along with the tape," said Wally.

"Did she say anything else?" said Eddie.

"Not much, just that she gave him some drugs to get him to confess on tape."

"I wonder if they hooked up," said Mikey.

"I doubt they did. Ruby said in Vegas all they did was listen to music while Mr. Awesome was fucked up," said Eddie.

"Good. He's married; he better not be cheating," said Mikey.

"I never thought he would. Figured he would just party and then take too many drugs and be a mess," said Eddie.

At 3:00 p.m., Mr. Awesome and Ruby arrived at the tour bus. Mr. Awesome looked like he'd been through a war. Dirty clothes, glasses crooked, a beard coming in, pants rolled up to the knees, showing no socks and even a wrong shoe.

"Rats, I am so glad there's no rally tonight. I desperately need a shower and some delicious food, followed by some relaxing in my room the rest of the night. See you tomorrow."

"So here's your tape," said Ruby. Around twenty minutes into it is where the good stuff is. And be nice to him; he's a sweet guy. Don't ruin his life that much."

"Yeah, well, that nice guy is a prick," said Eddie.

"Thanks again, Ruby," said Wally. "Here is your money, and please give two thousand dollars to Candy."

The Rats eagerly went into the bus to listen to the tape. They made sure Mr. Awesome was in the shower, and then they played the tape with the headphones on. Mikey and Wally each put an ear bud in their ear. Eddie could do nothing but read their facial expressions.

They fast-forwarded the tape to around the twenty-minute mark.

"So tell me about the pinball stuff that's going on—like, how did it all develop?"

"Rube a lube, can you keep a secret?"

"Of course, honey. Whatever you tell me goes into the vault. Client–customer confidentiality."

"Well, some really rich guys paid me a lot of money. I mean, a lot of money…cash, cash, so much cash, I couldn't say no. They said, 'Mr. President, here's all this money if you let us experiment with humans. Let us turn humans into animals.' Anything they wanted."

"So did they turn any humans into animals, then?"

"Yeah, they got some."

"Was it anybody you knew?"

"They asked me if I cared who they turned, and I knew this punk band who sang about how DC sucked, so I said, 'Take their singer, Johnny Piss Rat.' I hate what I did, Ruby. Those boys are really good people, and I allowed their singer to be turned into a rat. Then these rich guys asked if they could test new pills on people. And, Ruby, do you want to know what I said?"

"If you want to tell me, sure."

"I said, 'Sure.' As long they were responsible and I decide on how they will test the meds."

The Rats stopped the tape and then rewound it for Eddie to listen to.

"That fuckin' piece of shit," shouted a jagged, tattered Eddie, whose sullen brain demanded alcohol or else it would go on a strike.

"I can't believe it's official that Johnny is a rat. Our lead singer is a rat." Wally's brain kept repeating it over and over like a broken record. He felt nebulous and murky, like an octopus fresh out of ink.

The Piss Rats spent the next hour or so oozing venom. After their systems were detoxed from acrimony, they embarked upon the problem of how to confront Mr. Awesome.

"Well, first we need to call Carla. Any volunteers?" said Mikey.

"It's like calling parents and telling them their child has been killed," said Wally.

"Let me slam a beer, and I will do it," voiced Eddie.

"Next, how to deal with Mr. Awesome," Said Mikey.

They would wait until Carla landed to face off with the president. They wanted full control of every pinball warehouse in exchange for not announcing to the world that Mr. Awesome was really Mr. Corrupt. If he was as astute as his swagger suggested, they were sure he would comply. The Piss Rats would then be the proprietors of the pinball warehouses. No gods, no managers. They thought they would only hire punks to run the warehouses. But really, once they told Carla the lowdown, her voice would be the loudest.

Then they had to figure out how to cross paths with Johnny. Everyone had seen the rat around, but nobody ever discussed it or wanted to believe it could be Johnny. Ignorance is bliss.

Eddie called Carla and told her the news. She yelped and moaned as her soul began to leak out of her pores.

# IT'S TIME TO GO

The next morning Jed and Patti woke up, and urgently the measuring commenced. Another quarter inch put him now at six foot two.

Jed marched from the bedroom to the kitchen, where he tore open the cabinet and grabbed the sweetest thing he could find. He squeezed an entire bottle of agave syrup into his mouth. Then he took the vanilla extract and poured it in his mouth until he felt a revolt brewing in his stomach. Patti was outside the kitchen, just staring at her madman husband. He ingested every unhealthy ingredient he could find. When he could take no more, he wobbled past Ana as vomit oozed and gushed out of his mouth.

As the days and weeks passed, he kept growing and growing. Now at six foot seven inches, he said, "Patti, I love you and the kids more than anything, but I think I need to leave."

With tears streaming down her face, Patti said, "Where will you go? You can't just leave us! That's insane."

"The neighbors or kids will notice this, and once the authorities find out, its lights out."

"What if you just stay inside? I mean, you could see clients via Skype. There's just got to be a solution besides running away."

"Don't worry, Patti; I will be fine. I just need to lay low. I want to rid my body of whatever it is that's causing this growth. Since I believe it's stemming from my healthy habits, I think it's best I live a feral lifestyle for a bit. If I am still growing while living so rottenly, then we know it's not my superior health regimen."

"Well, I guess that makes sense, but where will you go?"

"There's a homeless settlement in the city. I want you to drop me off there tomorrow."

A crying Patti reluctantly agreed.

Patti dropped Jed off a few blocks away so he could walk to the homeless camp to make it look legit. Jed walked into the camp and surveyed his new surroundings. He detected that nothing healthy was happening there or had ever happened there. He entered the camp, and a few heads cocked upward with snarls and grunts. An older man moved his creaky bones and advanced toward him. Jed proceeded to act cautiously, with his hand seconds away from a knife in his pants pocket.

"Well, how you doing big guy?" asked the homeless man.

"I've had better days," chuckled Jed.

"Well, yeah, I think we all have had better days. Let me show you around."

The homeless man showed Jed around the camp. Jed couldn't believe he was leaving all the creature comforts one could ever desire and replacing them with minimal accommodations.

A guy and girl with dreadlocks walked up to him and offered him a swig from something in a paper bag. This was his first real test. Was he serious about leaving his optimal health regimen and engaging in every possible unhealthy habit? It felt like every eye in the camp was watching him. But that could be due to how tall he was. Denying the paper-bag beverage would raise doubts in their minds as to whether or not he was a legit homeless person. He reached his hands outward, and as he put the brown bag to his lips, he thought about his family and kids and swallowed it down. The taste was a mixture of iron and lemon. Tolerable but not enjoyable like his morning veggie and fruit drinks. He took another swig and handed it back, thanking them. His body felt a strange but pleasant vibration. Jed and his new friends drank from the brown bag for the remainder of the evening while others meandered in and out of the camp with other liquids and drugs.

He smoked weed as if it were something he'd done daily for years and years. When the crack showed up, he passed at first, but the drunker he got, the stronger his desire was to stop growing and go home to his family. He wanted to make sure he did everything possible to stop this growing, so he took two hits from the crack pipe. His head felt like it was stuck inside a moving fan. He still couldn't see how people ruined their lives for it, but he'd only taken two hits.

He woke up the next morning on a dirt floor with a pounding headache. He reached into his bag for some Tylenol. Thinking about last night's debauchery and today's rude awakening, he said with the wrath of a thousand cobras, "Take that, you stupid fucking body. No way you're growing now! I will do everything possible to starve you of all nutrients and anything healthy!"

He quickly pondered punching himself in the face to further inflict injury, but then a woman strolled up, offering him a cig and a swig from a malt liquor bottle. No need to ponder and be pensive about this anymore. Game on. He grabbed the bottle and took an aggressive chug and then lit up the cigarette.

"So what brings you here? By the way, my name is Nico."

"Nice to meet you, Nico. I lost my job. Then my wife and kids told me if I have no job and am going to be home all day, then I should just leave and let Mommy work on finding a replacement who can buy us shiny new things."

"Wow, that's brutal!"

"Yeah, it's one of the toughest things a man can encounter, having his wife and kids give him the boot over a normal life occurrence. So now I am here."

"Well, welcome." Nico handed him the malt liquor, and he took a generous swig, filling his entire mouth. His outlook immediately seemed to soften up. The cold gray sky seemed to speak to him: "Jed, everything will be OK if you just go with the flow. Let it all go…never say bye…always say hi…hey ho woah…let it be up tempo."

Jed walked around the camp and took part in everything he could find that was not healthy. He saw some people eating some questionable aging bread, and he walked over, asking for a taste. He noticed a speck of blue mold on it, and he knew this was what he needed right now. He then saw a group of people shooting up with some needles. That was the one thing he would never touch. A sure death sentence. He heard a noise and reached into his pocket for his phone. It was his wife. "Come home, please. We all miss you."

# LETDOWNS BARELY LET
# ME DOWN ANYMORE

Waiting for Carla was extremely stressful. First they had to convince Mr. Awesome to cancel or delay the next event in Phoenix. This involved Eddie pretending to get arrested for public drunkenness. Ava could tell something was up. She kept asking Mikey what was going on.

"Listen, Mikey, you asked to talk to Mr. Awesome in private at the hotel, and now you all look like you're about to blow a gasket. I know something is up. Just take a walk with me. It's gorgeous weather out. It will do you some good to let some fresh air and sun penetrate through your skin into the deepest, darkest parts of your soul."

Mikey finally succumbed to Ava's hog-tie and told her everything. She started crying and hugging Mikey.

"I am so sorry, Mikey. I can't believe he did that."

"Yeah, we're all still pretty jolted—like I don't think it's been fully digested yet that our singer is now a rat. Once Carla arrives, it will be intense, and I think we will then fully realize what's transpired."

They walked for an hour. Mikey was jealous of the weather since one of his favorite things in life was taking walks in beautiful weather, and LA had this weather most of the time, while Philly had maybe a hundred days a year that he labeled as perfect. He was constantly begrudging the CA weather. But he reminded himself that the fall season on the East Coast was truly a sight for the eyes. Those oranges, yellows, and reds were so vibrant and rich. Plus, they didn't have to worry about earthquakes or droughts. And with every day being so perfect, did people in California just take it for granted? When they got a beautiful day on the East Coast, they always appreciated every second of it.

They picked Carla up at LAX at 4:00 p.m. They asked if she was hungry, and she said she didn't have much of an appetite since she found out about Johnny. But she was feeling sluggish and wobbly, so some food was vital. They saw a Mexican restaurant ahead, and everybody agreed that burritos would be righteous.

The Rats knew they had to be delicate about the discussion of Johnny with Carla. She would act on raw gut emotions, which meant no compromise on inflicting maximum pain on Mr. Awesome. Slow torture. Eyeballs removed with rusty forks while cracking bones like kindling wood. The Rats had to show her in a soft, caring way that they agreed and wanted to do the same to Mr. Awesome, but it wasn't the wise, brainy way to handle it. Full control of the pinball warehouses in return, Mr. Asshole remains president and avoids prosecution. Carla would most likely want Mr. Asshole to spend eternity constantly drowning in waves of bright orange flames.

Midway through their meal, a distraught and weary Carla said, "So what are your plans for the president?"

Mikey talked first. "First of all, were all devastated over the news of Johnny being a rat. Obviously, you are heartbroken, and we want you to know, we will one hundred percent support whatever you want to do right now. What we were tentatively considering was approaching the president, telling him about the audio, and demanding full control over the thirty pinball manufacturing warehouses and talking to the losers who turned Johnny into a rat to see if they can reverse it. I know this may sound like a very light demand, but we thought about it all day and night. If we try to sue the president, then our lives are forever changed. We will be in court for years, and honestly, it's a punk band against the US government. The chances of them killing us within days of announcing this are very hefty. Handing over control of the pinball warehouses to us would benefit the punk community because we would only hire punks to work there.

Carla had tears streaming down her face as a flashback of her introduction to Johnny flashed through her brain. It was after a gig at the bar. He was walking past her and stopped to comment on her dress. He really dug the skulls and switchblade design on it. He asked if she'd purchased it from Sour Puss Clothing. She responded with "If you can guess where I got my shoes from, I will permit you a date with me." He removed her shoes and said, "What shoes?" He was so witty and straightforward. There was no pretense. *Finally, a real man,* she'd thought. Her soul mate. Now he'd become a rat.

She thought about their home and how they were planning on getting married in a few years and starting a family. Now it was just a pile of ashes to be blown away at the slightest hint of wind. A few more tears slid down her face. She then thought about what Mikey had told her. She knew it was true. The US government versus a punk band was a joke. Not only would they win, but most likely they would snuff them out instantly. Control and ownership of the pinball warehouses, modest as it was, at least it something that could maintain Johnny's legacy by only hiring punks.

"What if Mr. Awesome tries to kill us the moment we break the news? You don't become the most powerful person on the planet by allowing roadblocks to exist. You destroy all that's in your path without hesitation," whispered a defeated Carla.

"We already thought about that and have sent letters out to various family and friends explaining the situation, so he can't kill us because there are witnesses littered across the nation," said Wally.

"Well, if that's the case, why don't we sue him, since he can't kill us because you've already told others," said Carla.

"They would find who we sent those letters to and make their lives hell. They would stop at nothing. Most likely torture them. It would be awful," said Eddie.

She started to cry a little more and said, "I think we should talk to our parents and hire lawyers."

"We need to do this tomorrow, Carla. Any delays, and we risk the chance of him finding out somehow, and then we're screwed," said Mikey.

Anguish washed over her as she said, "I understand; do what you must."

# WHAT SIDE ARE YOU ON

"Mr. Awesome, this is Carla, Johnny's girlfriend. She flew out here after we told her that her beau and our lead singer was turned into a rat by the president of the United States," said Mikey.

Mr. Awesome lost all the color in his face. He cleared his throat and said, "Carla, I am sorry your boyfriend is missing, but I had nothing to do with it."

"Hey, Mr. Asshole, we have it on tape," shouted Eddie. He hit the play button. Mr. Awesome just stared out the window until they hit stop.

"I am so sorry; I just assumed punks were subhuman. That their lives were pointless. But after getting to know you guys, I found out you are great people who just have different viewpoints than the rest of us."

Carla's body began to spasm as she screamed, "You fuckin' piece of shit, you turned Johnny into a rat!" She then began attacking Mr. Awesome. Nobody, including Mr. Awesome, did anything.

He'd earned this via paper-thin morals and ethics so light a scale could not weigh them.

"Listen, asshole, here's how it goes down. We want full control over the pinball warehouses, and we want to talk with the people responsible for turning Johnny into a rat."

"And if I don't comply?"

Eddie held up the recorder.

"And we recorded it on a cell phone as well."

"For what it's worth, the original plan was to test the pharmaceuticals on you three. But after that first night, I saw that you guys were sincere and upright so I called Big Pharma in a drunken frenzy telling them the plan to test on you three was canceled. Within two hours, a man arrived and injected your hands with metal so the public instead of you guys would now be the victims of the experimental dosing. I was acting all weird and erratic because I was playing pinball to absorb the meds. I wanted the meds to twist and turn my brain into a mess so I could then with no more guilt then I already have, try and make myself hate you guys. If I could hate you, then I wouldn't care about what I did to you. Those pills are wicked though, one second I am fine, the next I am mentally mad. Have you told anybody else about this?"

"We have told a few close family and friends, so if you try to clip us now, it will go public. Your best bet is to continue the pinball tour as if nothing happened and give us full control of the warehouses. Then you will talk to the assholes who turned Johnny into a rat to see if they can reverse it," said Mikey. He looked over at Ava for support, and she held his hand.

"Understood. I think your proposition will work out. I will call my guys now about the rat problem."

"That's my fuckin' boyfriend! Have some respect, you fucker," shouted a rosey red bloodshot eyed Carla.

Mr. Awesome walked back to his room while Carla, Ava, and the Rats retreated to theirs. They were all comforting Carla when they heard a jar snap. A pack of rubbernecks peaked out to see Mr. Asshole making a peanut butter and jelly sandwich. He saw them peering at him, and he quietly muttered, "This phone call could take a while, and I am starving."

"So you said earlier, you think Johnny is around here...like, there have been rat sightings?" said Carla.

They all said they had seen a rat here and there and agreed that it must be Johnny.

"Well, how do we communicate with him, if we can. I mean, at least can I keep him as a pet?" The thought of keeping her boyfriend as a pet produced a liquid leak from her eyes.

"Now that you are here, Carla, I have faith he will appear very soon," said Eddie.

An hour later, Mr. Awesome called for Ava. After a minute of talking to him, Ava came back and told everybody that the head guy responsible for turning Johnny into a rat would be here tomorrow. The president had delayed a few stops on the tour. So for right now, they were just going to wait for this guy to appear.

Carla then asked, "Sorry, but who are you? Mikey's boyfriend or something?"

She blushed a little and said, "I am the president's assistant."

"So what side are you on, then?" asked Carla.

Ava had never really thought about that until now. She really didn't know. She had to keep her job with the president to protect her daddy, but she also was starting to have feelings for Mikey. "I am neutral," she proclaimed.

# KING OF PUNK ROCK

Dr. Lou from the pharmaceutical company landed early the next day. Immediately Carla quizzed him about the reversal of human to rat. "Miss, first, I am extremely sorry for this, and yes, we do have the ability to turn him back into a human. However, that technology has only been tested a dozen or so times. Yes, it's been successful, but I'm being pragmatic at this stage, which means I'm not exactly sure it will work."

Once he said this, a rat jumped on the coffee table. It felt like an earthquake erupting internally inside all who witnessed it. Carla put her arm out, and Johnny Piss Rat walked up to her arm in a casual, carefree, unrestrained movement, as if her arm was the Asbury Park boardwalk on an angelic summer afternoon. Once he reached the top of her shoulder, he perched there, quickly biting his leg to satisfy a pestering itch and then looking outward at the astonished humans.

The atmosphere in the room became dubious and wobbly. What was the next step? Did he understand English still? Would he attack them, piercing skin, causing scars and defects?

Carla blurted out, "Johnny, baby, are you OK? Do you need to see a doctor? Are you thirsty?"

The rat showed no emotion, indifferent to it all. A few times he moved, but only to adjust his position. Carla picked him up, kissed his head, and said, "Don't worry! We're going to turn you back into a human."

Finally showing a sign of life, Johnny's scant head moved left and then right.

"Did he just shake his head in response to her promise to turn him back to a human," said a puzzled Dr. Lou.

"His head definitely made the movement of one saying no," said Wally.

Carla asked him again. "Babe, do you want to stay a rat or transform back into a human?"

Again, the same mannerisms as before. Head to the left, then right. An avalanche of emotions rudely overcame Carla. Tears impolitely showed up and refused to vamoose. Instantaneously, Carla saw this as rejection. What had she done that was so rotten to garner treatment like this?

*It was the most grueling decision one can make. Remain a varmint. A creature seen in the world as one that should be exterminated. The lowest of low. A carrier of nothing but plagues and maladies. Subtraction, not addition. I cherished Carla and the Piss Rats, but the freedom associated with this black fur and four legs…well, it was something punks craved more than oxygen. No alarm clocks or hundreds of hours in a dirty tour bus. No money problems or worrying if my throat can handle another night screaming. No constantly trying to balance the band with Carla. I am going to miss being a human, but this is just too punk rock to pass up. Hand me the crown, I am the king of punk rock.*

Carla then dropped a bomb so intense it would turn humans and their fancy architecture into crispy fried onions.

"I demand to be turned into a rat. There's simply no way I can handle my soul mate being a pet. Cats and dogs are pets, not punk singers."

"Miss, take a few nights to think about this. It will be the biggest decision of your life."

"Fuck you! You don't think I know this?"

Infuriated and unable to sit any longer, Carla stood up. She momentarily thought about lunging at Dr. Lou. Two hands around his neck, squeezing until his face turned purple like an eggplant. As if letting go could cause her demise. Like a landlord evicting a tenant, she felt exposed and destitute. Swiftly, a door flew open, and out went the crestfallen Carla.

Wally said, "Give her some time to digest this calamity."

*Johnny's carefree, jovial mind felt a sensation it had yet to feel while covered in fur. A deeply rooted burden that instantly turned him into a nervous wreck. Guilt and joy colliding, causing massive injuries. If the procedure failed to produce optimal results, would Johnny ever be able to recover, knowing all the fingerprints on the crime scene pointed to him and only him? Was he selfish in this ultimate act of punk rock worship? But on the flip side, he wanted to frolic and boogie down in delighted grace at the thought of Carla joining him as a rat.*

The Piss Rats, Carla, and Ava chatted endlessly as darkness slowly replaced light and the clock went tick, tock, tick, tock, while Johnny hunkered down on Carla's shoulder. With still no definite answer on whether Johnny could understand them, but assuming he could from his head swingin' back and forth earlier, they discussed everything under the sun. Pros and cons were launched in every direction. Carla would be reunited with her boyfriend. Carla and Johnny could tour with the Piss Rats and be on stage the entire show. If that wasn't the most punk thing ever, they didn't want to know what was. What was their life span now going to be? If they had sex and Carla became pregnant, what kind of offspring would that yield? Would the government find out and want to steal them for experiments? What would Carla eat? Could she still consume alcohol?

Carla woke up the next morning and looked over on the dresser to witness what no woman should have to see: her man curled up like a shrimp in a little bed she'd made. Her empathy to the plight of Johnny's new existence would override any rational, logical thoughts. Intuition told her that the constant internal chaos was a waste. She would soon be side by side with her lover to face the world in the most unconventional of ways or die trying.

# AVA'S NO ANT

Ava's brisk walk quickly turned into a gallop. Adrenaline sped through her trim torso. With the Piss Punk's discovery of Mr. Awesome's underhanded act of betrayal, her master plan to protect Daddy was now compromised. Her great plan ruined by a bunch of punks! Although she might have chemistry with one of them. Her nervous energy was now overflowing like a bowl left out during a hurricane. Her brain was a locomotive with no breaks, replaying over and over in her mind how it all commenced. She was spending night and day trying to orchestrate a plan that would put her in a position to influence people of authority. Government or law enforcement was ideal. She'd decided she would clandestinely discover top-secret information that she would keep in the vault, only to be released if her daddy was arrested. Then, something that made the hair on her arms rise when she reflected upon it—blackmail.

She'd first started working as an aide to the senator of Virginia. After a year, she began to get frustrated. She had zero access to confidential material. Every visit to her parents' place saw oodles of shiny new objects. A new car, a new boat, new tits for Mommy. Daddy was making tons of money, which only meant he would be busted soon. She'd seen enough movies to know that the ones at the top were either clipped by the ones below or busted in a sting operation. Something had to happen immediately. Her rise up the corporate ladder was slower than a morphine drip. She knew the president's assistant's name. That was a start, she concluded. Days turned into weeks and then into months. It felt like being hand-cuffed to a radiator.

Luck finally found her side when at a museum one Sunday, try-ing to calm her mind, she spotted the president's assistant with her husband. Knowing this would be her only chance to do something, she followed her into the bathroom. Having no plan at all, she just let it unfold naturally, letting emotions and instinct guide the way. As the president's assistant was washing her hands, Ava said while quickly flashing a gun, "My father is a Mob boss, and if you don't take a leave of absence and have me replace you, he will destroy everything you love."

After a month on the job as the president's assistant, she decided it was time to strike like a cobra. The first time she suggested they get a drink, he thought she was coming on to him, so she made up that she had a boyfriend but it wasn't that serious. This way the president's brain would conclude that he had a chance to hook it with her. Her experience as an attrac-tive female taught her that if guys thought they had any chance of hooking up with you, they would hang with you. The first few times out, Mr. Awesome was conservative with his alcohol intake, so she needed to find a way for him to let loose. Remove the brakes and speed limit signs. She decided to add some shots to the mix as well as wear a shirt that showed generous cleavage. Results were obvious. Speech more liberal. Volume intensified. But still, no sensitive information would pour out of his mouth like water from a spigot.

Confused and frustrated, she'd spent many restless nights pondering it all. Finally, it struck her, and she felt silly for it taking this long to figure out. Was she not her father's daughter? It was time to see if being a gangster was part of her genetic makeup.

She knew Mr. Awesome's schedule and identified the times when he was vulnerable. After his Tuesday night briefings with intelligence officials, Ava knew he would always drive himself to a local deli that opened up just for him. Nobody knew he did this, not even his security team. He always told them he was showering, but it provided him with a rare break from everything. True autonomy.

As he was leaving the car, Ava put a gun to his head. Wearing a voice disguise box, she told him to get back into the car. In the back seat, Ava, wearing a black face mask, told Mr. Awesome he had five minutes to tell her about the undercover stuff he was involved in. She had no idea if he was involved in anything, but this was her only plan. Clearing his throat and searching for some salvia to quench his dry mouth, he began, "Well, the pharmaceutical companies have offered me millions and millions if I give them approval to do whatever they want, but I'm just not sure it's a good idea."

Ava was perplexed. So he might do it? What the hell. Confused as to what to do next, she said, "Well, why don't you tell them they can go about it slowly and check in with you on everything they do. If there is anything you don't like or approve of, they can stop."

"You know, that's not a bad idea."

"So you're going to do it, then?"

"Well, I guess so."

Ava could not believe how strange this was going.

"I think you should seriously consider it."

"OK, maybe I will."

Concluding that this was the most bizarre stickup ever, she opened the car door and did her best to blend in with the night.

# WALL OF WEIRDOS

Like a famished lion awake from slumber and on hunt for prey, the Piss Rats began a process unfamiliar to them. Finding a new singer. Even when they began as a band, they never had to audition a singer; it just naturally happened with the greatest of ease. Now it would be mechanical and cold. Monotonous discussions and audits of each potential candidate's pros and cons.

Wally's phone reverberated inside his jeans. He dug into his pocket and retrieved the phone, and an eerie wave of crimson spread across his face, as he felt like he recognized the phone number

"Hello?"

"Oh, hey, Gay Wally, it's Candy."

Confused as to why she was calling, he just said, "Oh…um… hey, Candy, what's up?"

"I want to try out for the singer of your band."

"Ha-ha-ha. Really? You can sing?"

"Don't patronize me, Wally; just let me prove it."

"OK, Candy. Let me check with the guys and get back to you."

"Listen, you nincompoop, I am trying out. Case closed. So just text me a time and place. If you fail at this, our next S&M session will not be as friendly."

As she hung up, Wally thought about his baseball dad and sick mom and Alice, and for a few seconds, it felt amiable and attractive.

"So, guys, remember that stripper Candy? Well, she wants to try out next week."

"Wally, come on man; this is serious. Just tell her we found a singer," said Eddie.

"Holy shit, guys," said Mikey. "I just had a ferocious idea of our band with her as the singer. Fuck, damn. OK, she's definitely trying out. Can you picture her as the singer with Carla and Johnny sitting on each of her shoulders while she sings? Fuckin' primitive and striking!"

# LET THE RIVER FLOW

B ack at home surrounded by all his creature comforts, seven-foot-five Jed was ecstatic to be back with his family. However, the joy he felt was constantly in conflict with his brain over his height issue. He would be playing with his kids and loving every second of it, only to have it be ruined when out of nowhere severe depression would show up like a long-lost friend in the middle of the night with nowhere else to go. And of course, the door was wide open.

A week after he'd come home, Jed and Patti were preparing dinner together when she mentioned that she had talked to her brother Eddie a few weeks ago. They got to talking, and she was a bit liberal in her speech from a couple glasses of wine and broke down and told him about the height issue. Before Jed had a chance to flip out over her releasing information that could put their entire family in jeopardy, she told him Eddie promised to never tell anybody.

"Anyway, as we got to talking more and more, Eddie mentioned that if you were looking for a place to hide out and not be healthy, you were welcome to go on tour with the Piss Rats and be their roadie."

The Piss Rats' gut reaction to Jed was the obvious one. "That's a big dude."

"So, Jed, we heard you play the saxophone?"

"Yeah, I played in middle school a little."

"What if we incorporated the sax into some of our songs live? I mean, we don't need to record with a sax, but a seven-foot-five sax player who most likely will be eight feet soon—it would just intensify our already towering stage persona," said Wally.

It felt like a lightning strike directly into his brain, hearing those revolting words.

Eight feet tall.

"So you have no idea what's causing this growth, Jed?" said Mikey.

Before Jed spoke, he reached into his bag and pulled out a canister of whipped cream. The Piss Rats thought, *Is he making a sundae or something?* When he put the white tip into his mouth and no vanilla ice cream, caramel, or cherries appeared, they knew there was no sundae-making here; just a man getting a quick, intense high that was labeled in the party scene as a "whippet." Jed gazed at the Piss Rats for thirty seconds in a deep haze, fully paralyzed from the lack of oxygen reaching his brain. Finally, he said, "No clue. I thought it was my personal health regimen. I was extremely healthy and took lots of supplements. So I figured it was that. But after I started smoking crack and eating moldy bread and sleeping on dirt, I continued to grow, so I guess it's not that. But just in case it is, I am doing my best to use and abuse my body." Jed reached into his pocket and extracted a handful of bright-orange candies and launched them into his mouth. Trying to chew and talk at the same time, he said, "I can't wait to party with you guys. Eddie, I've heard stories about you!"

Eddie, never one to be out partied, thought to himself that if he ever felt a bit restrictive with partying, then Jed was sent from God himself to remove the handcuffs and let the river flow.

"So, Jed, would you be open to playing a few songs on your sax with us live in addition to being our roadie? We still need to discuss it privately as a band, but right now we're pretty open to the idea," said Wally.

Jed thought about being on stage. It was the opposite of what he wanted right now. He wanted to hide away and not have a bright light showcasing his freakish body. But he also felt like the Piss Rats were so cool to bring him into their family. Always being a firm believer in family, Jed concluded that he would just cut his hair or wear some makeup to disguise himself.

"Sure, we can give it a try," said Jed. He then saw an ant crawling on his arm and ate it.

"Awesome. We will let you know what we decide. Also, did you ever play any pinball in that new pinball manufacturing warehouse in Chicago," asked Mikey.

"As a matter of fact, yes, I did. I found the entire concept quite slapstick but also refreshing and whimsical."

The Piss Rat's bodies shook and trembled. Could the pills released by the pinball machines have caused this? It was very possible. And if so, who else was having body morphing issues?

# CHARLIE

The Piss Rats and Jed were walking to get some food when they saw a guy in the alley crawling on all fours like an animal. A sense of compassion bulldozed through their bodies from their experience with Johnny.

"Hey, are you OK, man? Do you need some food or help?"

The man arose from all fours and spoke in a coherent and civilized manner.

"I am fine, just minding my own business. Don't want any trouble."

"Neither do we, man. We just want to make sure you're OK. Seriously, we just want to talk with you. We're not cops or anything; we're a punk band."

The man appeared to lighten up upon hearing this. "Well, that's very kind of you. How about we hit up a bar instead of this dirty alley?" said the man.

They sat at a small wooden table and ordered some beers.

"So what's your name?" said Wally.

"Charlie."

"Well, it's nice to meet you, Charlie. My name is Wally. That's Eddie, Mikey, and Jed. We play in the Piss Rats."

"The what?" asked Charlie.

"Our band is called the Piss Rats."

"Oh, OK, I understand."

"The concept for the name was originally rooted in the phrase 'rat race,' which I am sure you're familiar with." Charlie nodded. "Anyway, not to get too in-depth, we then wanted to call our band the Pissed Rats. Like we're angry that adult life forces you to act like a rat in a race—just work, work, work and go, go, go. But the Piss Rats flows better," said Eddie.

"So we noticed you crawling on all fours in that alley, but it looks like you're not a screwball or infected with rabies," said Mikey.

"You are correct. I have a job and an apartment and live a conventional life, but last week I started getting the urge to crawl like an animal. And when I say urge, I mean, I absolutely must do it."

With tears starting to form in his eyes, he continued. "So in the evening when the sun's sleeping, I find alleys and act out my animal instincts. I just don't understand what's happening to me."

The Piss Rats all looked at one another, and then Eddie told Charlie that they needed to have a quick band meeting.

The Piss Rats walked outside, and they all began talking at the same time.

"This sounds like the same shit that's happened to Johnny and Jed," said Wally in a frenzied tone.

"I am positive this guy is suffering from similar afflictions as Johnny and Jed," said Eddie.

"We have to try to explain to him that we know what's happening without compromising the safety of our crew," said Mikey.

"Mikey is correct. I feel it's our obligation to try to help him after what has happened to Johnny and Jed," said Wally.

As the Piss Rats walked back into the bar, they could feel their nihilistic tendencies slowly being replaced with those of parental

care. If there were more people out there in pain and embarrassment, they would do everything in their power to nourish them
and help them return from their withered state.

"So, Charlie, we can't exactly tell you many details for our own
safety, since we just met you and don't know if you will talk to the
cops. But we will tell you that you are not the only one experiencing random body modifications or strange urges, and we would
like to help you out as well as offer you a job. So what we're thinking is the following. You would tour with us, and every city we go
to, it would be your job to try to find more people who are dealing
with similar issues to what you are experiencing. I know it's asking a lot of you to just drop your job and everything to tour with a
punk band on the assumption that there are more people like you
out there, so take a few days to think about it and let us know. Also,
if it turns out you can't find anybody, we'll make sure you still have
a job in our organization one way or another."

"That's a lot to digest—wow. So basically, if I want a chance at
finding out what's happening to me, then I need to blindly trust a
bunch of punks I just met on the street?"

"I know this is the dictionary definition of the word 'shady,' but
yes, you are correct. As for solving your affliction and seeking out
revenge and justice, we offer no guarantees of that happening. In
fact, we want you to go into this venture assuming that will never
happen. Your job is to simply try to find more people who are suffering and let them know they will always have a home with the
Piss Rats. If you reject our proposal, but still want to be involved
with us you can work at one of our pinball warehouses or still tour
with us and maybe sell merch or do security or something."

Charlie was hoping that "something" didn't mean using him
as a novelty act to run across the stage on all fours while they were
playing like some kind of freak. He was not a freak, he reassured
himself. He just had this urge he had to act upon a few times daily.
He would not allow this to defeat him.

"OK, what is your number? I will think about it and let you know."

As the Piss Rats and Charlie parted ways, they watched him transform from human to animal as he raced into an alley.

Charlie texted them the next morning.

"So, Charlie, once we park the tour bus, you then start walking around the city, keeping your eyes and ears open looking for more people afflicted with mysterious body modifications or anything else that doesn't look normal. This will be tough, because most people—if there are more people like you and Jed—are hiding away in their homes. Too embarrassed to leave their houses and trying to avoid the public at all costs. That being said, though, they do need to come out eventually, and we hope and pray you will be able to seek and find them when they do. Then, of course, once you find them, explain to them what we explained to you when we first found you," said Wally.

# FIRST UNITARIAN CHURCH

Their first gig was a sold-out show in the First Unitarian Church in their hometown of Philly. Word had spread throughout the city that the Piss Rats were back with a stripper as the lead singer.

The Piss Rats wanted this to be the punk show of the decade in Philly. They begged and pleaded for some older bands who didn't play anymore or played very rarely to join the gig. "Holy fucking shit," said Eddie. "We've convinced 2.5 Children Inc., the Boils, Kid Dynamite, Dis Sucks, Violent Society, Atom And His Package and Plow United to play at our show!"

"I don't get it, man. Like, how did you convince some of the best bands in Philly punk history to play our show? I mean, it's not even a record release show. It just a hometown show premiering a new singer," commented a puzzled but delighted Mikey.

"Dude, I don't know. I've just been running my mouth constantly about how our lead singer is a stripper and how the Piss Rats don't give a shit about anything anymore. We're here to plunder and pillage. Lock your windows and bolt your doors. Fuck you; punk rules. This is the new dawn of punk. Oddly, I am against all that. I hate having a stripper as our singer; it distracts from the music, and it's not punk. That being said, I also knew this was the only chance to ever see some of my favorite bands one last time. So basically, this show is all about feeding my personal obsessions. Don't hate, Mikey; I swear, don't fuckin' hate. In fact, this might just become my new hobby. Convincing my favorite retired bands to play reunion shows with us. Can you imagine a lineup of Avail, Fifteen, Fugazi, Sex Pistols, Operation Ivy, Against All Authority, His Hero His Gone and Crass?"

At 10:00 p.m., the Rats came on. Hysteria spread like a wildfire at the sight of the Piss Rats' new singer. Walloping breasts that the tiny ripped shirt could barely contain. Tattoos so generous that normal skin tone was rare. And then to top it all off, a rat on each shoulder. The easily offended and weak-stomached ones fled swiftly. The curious-minded ones simply took a few steps back and reached for their phones to document the never-before-seen spectacle. While the fearless hooligan ones couldn't get close enough to the action. Carla rocked a red Mohawk and red tail, while Johnny had a bright blue Mohawk and white tail.

In the middle of the set, Candy Piss Rat told the audience that a new song would be next. She wanted to add "about the last few months of our lives," but that was akin to summoning evil. People would connect the dots, and the Piss Rats would be expired and thrown in the dumpster for gutter punks to find and even dismiss. The crowd had heard about the president and pinball manufacturing but didn't know the relationship the Piss Rats had with these events, and it needed to stay that way. They only took the risk because the way the chorus rhymed and sounded was simply to great to pass up.

Candy said, "I am going to tell you the chorus now so you can sing along.

"'We are the Pinball Punks, politicians stink like skunks.'"

The crowd chanted the chorus" "We are the Pinball Punks, politicians stink like skunks…Pinball Punks, politicians stink like skunks!"

Then the band brought out its secret weapon. Seven-foot-five Jed came out wearing a kilt and nothing else. He belted and wailed on his sax while the entire building sang, "Pinball Punks, politicians stink like skunks."

As the last sounds of guitar and drum reverberated through the grimy walls, the Piss Rats felt a sense of bombast and jubilation for what music can truly contribute to society as they peered into the crowd of sweaty smiles and awesome admiration. In this calm Zen-like moment, Candy gathered enough fortitude to tell her bandmates that she had a new song she'd been working on that she wanted to play acoustically. The band didn't want to argue and cause a scene that would slow down this perfect evening, and they also craved a few minutes to regroup. So they gave her the go-ahead. Candy eyeballed the crowd, and they were chomping at the bit for more punk. She would have to make this one quick as to not lose the crowd's energy. She adjusted her acoustic guitar and noticed a piece of rose-colored dirt next to her boots. It reminded her of being a teenager and her mom pinning a rose on her dress before prom, but she quickly squashed and sterilized it. Rearview mirrors do nothing but slow you down. Carpe diem. She announced to the crowd, "This is another new one. Autobiographical. It's called Anxiety."

I don't know why
I am so wound up today
Could it be the dirt beneath my feet
Our eyes when we first meet
I don't know why
I am so wound up today
Could it be the books that don't get read

Listen to the records when I'm dead
I don't know why
I'm so wound up today
*Anxiety, anxiety*
*Anxiety when the sun's not up*
*Anxiety when leaders corrupt*
*Anxiety, anxiety, anxiety*
I don't know why
I am so wound up today
Could it be private property
And no trespassing signs for you and for me
I don't know why
I am so wound up today
Could it be the books that don't get read
Listen to the records when I'm dead
I don't know why
I'm so wound up today
*Anxiety, anxiety*
*Anxiety when the sun's not up*
*Anxiety when leaders corrupt*
*Anxiety, anxiety, anxiety*
I don't know why
I am so wound up today
Could it be the letter I found yesterday
The needle is always an exit sign
Never had a chance to say goodbye
I don't know why
I am so wound up today
Could it be the books that don't get read
Listen to the records when I'm dead
I don't know why
I'm so wound up today
*Anxiety, anxiety*

*Anxiety when the sun's not up*
*Anxiety when leaders corrupt*
*Anxiety, anxiety, anxiety*
I don't know why
I am so wound up today
Was it the alcohol inside of me
I try and try
But I need it sometimes to just see and be
I don't know why
I am so wound up today
Could it be credit cards and shitty front yards
I don't know why
I am so wound up today
Could it be the books that don't get read
Listen to the records when I'm dead
I don't know why I'm so wound up today
*Anxiety, anxiety*
*Anxiety when the sun's not up*
*Anxiety when leaders corrupt*
*Anxiety, anxiety, anxiety*

It was tough to decipher whether the crowd enjoyed the song, but it felt like therapy to Candy. Jed came out with his sax and played the last few lines of the song with Candy.

It was almost time for the curtains to close. Nobody wanted the evening to end and have reality punch them in the face. In the middle of the last song, Johnny plunged off Candy's shoulder and landed on all fours. Careful to not get stepped on and ruin the ace night, he skedaddled over to Eddie and opened his mouth. In the excitement and drunken haze, Eddie began pissing into Johnny's mouth. Johnny didn't move or run away. The crowd became ferocious at the barbaric and sadistic act of entertainment. Punk legends were born.

The post show was an electric buzz. Did Eddie really piss into that rat's mouth? Maybe that rat was their ex–lead singer, Johnny? Was it planned? Will they do it again? Who was that huge man wearing a kilt?

"Holy fuckin' shit, what the hell was that, Eddie?" uttered Mikey.

"Dude, I have no fuckin' clue what's going on right now. I just know Johnny came over and opened his mouth, and well, let's face it: we are called the Piss Rats. It all just kinda made sense in that manic moment."

Candy walked in with the two rats on each shoulder smoking a cig and holding a whiskey bottle. "Well, that was certainly interesting. Can't say I expected to see Eddie piss into Johnny's mouth."

They all looked at Johnny and Carla for some kind of explanation, but none was established. Two blank stares.

"I am calling Dr. Lou tomorrow to see if he can shed some light on this," said Mikey.

Later that night on the tour bus, Candy and Wally sat drinking some whiskey, joking, and reminiscing about the first night they met.

"It feels like forever ago," said Candy.

"Do you miss stripping and your life before the Piss Rats?"

"Not one bit. I feel like this could be my calling. On stage with Johnny and Carla on each shoulder, the crowd singing along—it truly is a natural, healthy form of Ecstasy that I get to feel almost every night. Also, I have been thinking and Candy is now dead. Moving forward, it's my birth name of Candace. It feels so great to trash Candy. When I first started stripping, the sleazy boss said upon hearing my name of Candace, 'Your new name will be Candy. People will want to eat you like Candy.'"

Wally's entire body seemed to hiccup upon hearing that. Refusing to allow his brain yet again to analyze the past month, he told himself he felt great hanging with Candace. Fuck everything and everybody who had a problem with it.

She grabbed Wally's shirt and pulled him close, and they kissed and kissed and didn't even stop when Eddie decided to pull up a chair and watch them. Finally, they paused to tell Eddie he was a supreme creep, before going to Candace's room for privacy.

Patti and the kids came backstage, excited to see their father. "Hey, guys, it's so great to see you. Did you have a good time tonight?" asked the mammoth human.

"Yes, Daddy; you were so great"

"Were you nervous?" asked Patti.

"Extremely nervous, yes, but it was a lot of fun. Kids, go say hi to Uncle Eddie while Daddy talks to Mommy."

As the kids walked away, Jed imagined them talking to a therapist about their problems and how it all began the night they saw Uncle Eddie piss into a rats mouth.

"I miss you so much," said Patti. "What are your thoughts so far about your new job?"

"It's certainly different from my last job. Honestly, I am actually enjoying it and I feel safe. That's the key right now. But I still don't know what's causing me to grow. It seems to have slowed down a bit," said Jed as he lit up five cigs at once, engulfing the room with toxic smoke.

They continued talking, now unable to see each other from all the smoke produced by Jed. "So I am seven foot nine now, growing about a quarter inch every few weeks."

Patti quickly interrupted him. "Please, let's not talk about your height. I am confident you will be fine."

They then talked for the next hour about the kids and the house.

# HOPE SPRINGS ETERNAL

Mikey called Dr. Lou at 10:00 a.m. the next morning. "Hey, this is Mikey. We met last month with Mr. Awesome. Do you have a few minutes to talk?"

"Sure, Mikey, what's up?"

"Well, last night at our gig, our guitarist pissed into Johnny's mouth. I am sure you remember that Johnny is a rat. Anyway, Eddie, our guitarist, pissed into Johnny's mouth, but we all swear that Johnny wanted it. Like he craved it. How could this be?"

Mr. Awesome's guy sighed, and a sense of frustration could be heard in his voice. "I told Mr. Awesome you guys would find out, but he insisted on me not telling you this."

"Telling us what!" shouted Mikey.

"Well, after Mr. Awesome picked out Johnny as a candidate for the human-to-animal experiment, he asked if we could also have his food source be urine."

Mikey should have gone ballistic. Darting at breakneck speed to find Mr. Awesome and unleashing his tension on easily breakable appendages. Instead, he just digested it like it was a healthy piece of food. He had a feeling his life would now consist of never-ending bullshit like this, and why let it mentally and physically warp you?

"He thought it would be a hilarious act of tomfoolery since your band name is the Piss Rats," said Dr. Lou. A tiny part of Mikey jumped for joy since their punk credentials were now off the charts, surpassing Sid Vicious and perhaps even GG Alien.

"What did he say?" asked Eddie.

"He said that Mr. Awesome thought it would be funny to have Johnny drink urine as his food source."

"What the fuck!" shouted Eddie.

Everyone was in shock.

"That is gross," said Ava.

The following day, there was a band meeting.

"So we need to figure out what direction to take the band," said Wally. "We've always prided ourselves on the fact that the Piss Rats is a no gimmick or shtick punk band. Let the music do the talking. So do we want to now incorporate Johnny into our live performance? You know, pissing in his mouth? The crowd absolutely loved it, and that's all the scene is talking about now. I feel like we almost have to run with it."

"Yeah, I think we have to do it," said Mikey. "What do you think, Eddie?"

Eddie's punk side was absolutely elated at the thought of pissing into Johnny's mouth. He'd finally reached the top of punk mountain or some shit like that. But on the flip side, how would Clash and his parents react to this? What if he ever needed to get a real job? Would they hire *"that weird punk who spent years pissing into his ex–lead singer's rat mouth"*? But in the end, it had to be done. He reluctantly knew that. To pass up an opportunity like this would haunt him forever. He was great at bullshitting, so he figured if this ever came back to mess with him, he could and would find ways to flip it around. Hope springs eternal.

"Johnny and Carla can squat on my shoulders while I sing too," said Candace.

Wally kissed Candace on the cheek and said, "I love how you're OK with all this—just so badass."

"Next, what about Jed? And what if Charlie finds more people like Jed? It sounds like there could be lots of people like him hiding away from the world, too freaked to come out."

"I think we take it case by case."

"Honestly, if Charlie finds one more person or three hundred more people, we're not turning them away. We have the resources available to help them. Each person will be analyzed and placed in the proper position of their comfort," said Wally.

"What about the pinball warehouses?" said Mikey. "We want all the employees to be punks, but how do we conduct a hiring process? Just because somebody says they're a punk doesn't mean they really are."

They all muttered and spat out different options, none of which seemed satisfactory. Then Eddie casually said, "What if we play punk songs? And if they can identify the band and album it came from, they are hired."

"Holy shit, Eddie's brain still works and works quite well," commented Wally.

"Sorry, Wally, we can't all have X stripper girlfriends we have already paid twenty thousand dollars toward."

"Yeah, real funny. What it take ya to come up with that one, two weeks?"

"Shut up, you two. Jeez, just stop it. Eddie's idea is solid as concrete, and we're going with that," said Mikey.

"So if we now own thirty warehouses, we need to hire managers ASAP," said Wally.

"Let's all reach out to our punk friends and spread the word that we are hiring," said Mikey.

"Let me do the hiring process, guys," said Ava who apparently was eavesdropping "If anybody finds out a punk band now owns all these warehouses, suspicion will rise, and you guys will be busted."

"Very smart, Ava. Thanks," said Mikey.

"This is going to be a huge endeavor, guys. I mean, we're pretty much going to be touring endlessly now that everyone wants to see us live," said Eddie.

"This is exactly why I believe we can do it, though, Eddie. We only have to work one hour a day; that leaves the rest of the day for us to work on getting the warehouses operational and functional. And really, if we hire solid punks as managers, our involvement will hopefully be minimal," said Mikey.

"Newsbreak, Mikey, we need to release an album pretty much after this tour is done, which means practicing every day," said Eddie.

"OK, fine, but we still have the time. Trust me, it will work."

"If we keep finding more Jeds and Charlies out there, they can also work in the warehouses. I know we want punks only. But I think we can make an exception here," said Ava.

They all agreed with Ava. If they were truly going to help others out, they would need jobs. Pinball warehouses would be the ideal spot.

# PINBALL PUNKS POLITICIANS
# STINK LIKE SKUNKS

The American tour started in New York. The Piss Rats were astounded at the lineup. All their favorite bands they never once expected to tour with. Night Birds, Strung Out, Ignite, Who Killed Spikey Jacket, The Slackers, and Crazy Spirit. It sold out in hours. Even with this impeccable lineup, it wasn't because of the music. Nobody really cared about that. What they did care about, what they absolutely craved, was the spectacle that was the Piss Rats' live show.

They had not announced that Johnny was a rat and his girlfriend Carla also a rat. They had no intention of ever disclosing that. Leaving it a mystery added an extra layer to their persona. Plus, as with aliens, the people could not handle the truth. When asked in endless interviews about how a stripper with a rat on each shoulder ended up replacing their singer, all they would say is, "You never know how life will turn out, and Johnny is always with us."

Sweat dripped and drizzled off the anxious crowd as they waited in the September heat for the Piss Rats to start strumming and
swatting at their instruments. They opened with "Years and Years."

I'm always thinking about Wissahickon Park
That river running east inside my heart
Cause the north is just skyscrapers, the south competition
The west is all the same
Nothing for me
Nothing for me
So I let my mind just drift away
Think about cheaper and slower days
Think about when life was just four walls and three meals
*I collect records*
*I collect scars*
*I always run, and I get far*
*I collect records*
*I collect scars*
*I always run, and I get far*
Broke down, not broken
Shaking but feeling
Broke down, not broken
Shaking but feeling
So my friend
What happened to those days
Those cheaper and slower days
When a train ride to the Troc was seven now fifteen
When a slice of pizza was a dollar now two or three
When what was ours was ours to keep
When what was ours was ours to keep
*I collect records*
*I collect scars*
*I always run, and I get far*

*I collect records*
*I collect scars*
*I always run, and I get far*
Broke down, not broken
Shaking but feeling
Broke down, not broken
Shaking but feeling
76 is broke again
Nothing moves
Nothing ends
The kids are all wild in the streets
The cities laugh in defeat
Give them space to create
Watch a town rise from hate
And watch a town rise from hate
Looking for leadership in you
Just a clown with no clue
When the sky is black and blue
Then your hero is not true
*I collect records*
*I collect scars*
*I always run, and I get far*
*I collect records*
*I collect scars*
*I always run, and I get far*
Broke down, not broken
Shaking but feeling
Broke down, not broken
Shaking but feeling
The leaves are orange, yellow, red
Soon will be dead
Winter gray and that slow decay
Tonight, I will lay low

Figure out which way to go
Cause I know that
Life makes sense
When streetlights and billboards
Are all burned out
And all that's left is the thoughts
Inside of my mind
I collect records
I collect scars
I will meet you in the car
Put our hands behind the wheel
We'll drive for years and years
Put our hands behind the wheel
We'll drive for years and years
We'll drive for years and years
We'll drive for years and years
We'll drive for years and years

The crowd responded enthusiastically to all the songs, but what they really wanted to hear was "Pinball Punks."

The Rats were now closing with that song. The last chorus saw Johnny climb down from Candace's shoulder and crawl toward Eddie. As Candace, Mikey, and the crowd sang, "We are the Pinball Punks, politicians stink like skunks," Eddie proceeded to piss into Johnny's mouth. The crowd went apeshit. Eddie hid behind his large amp, so the only thing seen was Eddie's face and liquid going into Johnny's mouth. Then Johnny climbed back on Candace's shoulder and watched the crowd go wild, letting his brain cells conjure up different thoughts about his current predicament.

*You never really know how life will turn out. One day you're singing for your band, living with your girlfriend, planning a future, and then the next day you're a rat, sitting on the shoulder of a stripper who replaced you as singer of your band. While your hard-core anti everything drummer is dating that striper. Then your band reaches its plateau from pissing into a rat's mouth. What if this all falls apart tomorrow? Then what? I must silence these thoughts and live for today*

Jed was so amped about the few times he was on the stage with his sax that he'd been practicing other ways to get up there. After the fifth song, when the Piss Rats needed a break, Jed strolled out and shot-gunned two beers and then smashed them into his head. If a little blood appeared, he smeared it all over his face. At the end of the set, he came out riding a unicycle. His plan of figuring out how to get on the stage as much as possible was proving to be a success. It was the ultimate rush for him.

After the show, they found Charlie talking with a girl named Lucy. They all introduced themselves, and Lucy told the band how much she loved their set and how much their music meant to her. As they were all hanging out and talking, the Piss Rats noticed that Lucy's eyes were changing colors every few minutes. Red to purple to blue to black. Mikey grabbed Charlie while the others continued talking to Lucy.

"Dude, great job; you already found somebody."

"What do you mean? She's completely normal."

"Did you happen to see her eyes changing colors?"

"Um no, I must have missed that. I mean, it was dark for your set. So once it ended, we just got to talking about how great a live set the Piss Rats are now."

"Oh, OK, I understand. So here is where you talk with her and find out what's going on. Actually, we might as well all do it now."

Mikey walked back to the others and bluntly said to Lucy, "When did your eyes start rotating different shades?"

Her face blushed, showing signs of embarrassment. Tears in the eye ducts began their march, looking to exit onto her face. "It started last week," she admitted, and then she immediately put her sunglasses on. "I have been calling out of work and wearing sun-glasses. After the show had ended tonight, I forgot to put them back on, and now you guys know my secret. Please don't tell anybody. I am so nervous. My eyes change colors according to my mood and the mood of the environment around me." She took off her glasses and asked them to tell her what color her eyes were now.

"Black," they all said.

"Black means I am scared and in danger. Somebody tell me a joke or say something funny."

"What's up with the phrase Civil War? Like is it really civil? 'Pardon me my good man, I wonder if I might trouble you for just a moment. I was planning on killing you and your whole family in the most brutal fashion imaginable in the next three minutes. I'm in quite a hurry so would you mind not defending yourself so I might go about my business in a expedited manner. Thanks so much.' If that actually is how it happens, then sure Civil War is fine, if not, maybe change it to Rude War?"

They all laughed

"What color are they now?"

"Orange."

"They turn orange when I am relaxed and content."

"Lucy, something is happening to people. That big guy on stage: he was five foot eleven a few months ago. I have the urge to get on all fours like a puma and run until the urge is gone. Here is my phone number; we can't offer you anything to help reverse your kaleidoscope eyes, but if you feel like you can't live life this way, you will always have a home with the Piss Rats."

The Piss Rats were impressed with Charlie's pitch. He was clear and honest, and there was sincerity in his language.

"Not quite sure I understand, guys. I mean, should I be that nervous about my eyes? I know something is not quite right with me, but to drop everything and join your parade, really?

"Lucy, if hospitals and the FBI discover your eyes changing color, there's a chance they will lock you in a cage and do endless experiments on you. So you need to be very cautious. We are offering you security, basically. We can't heal you or offer you an explanation for your predicament, but we can offer you a job and family. You do not need to be alone on this. Charlie is responsible for finding more people like you and offering them jobs. You would either work in the pinball warehouses or be out on tour with us, whatever works best for everybody," said Mikey.

# FINAL COMMUNIQUE

Wally was at the store gathering vegetables like a squirrel getting acorns when he felt his phone make a sound. He casually grabbed it and using muscle memory clicked to read the new text message.

"Wally, this is Wendy. I know that was you protecting the president in Chicago. I saw your star tattoo. Only you have that tattoo because it has my fuckin' initials on it! I am responsible for that small group that surrounded you and the president to cease fighting. Without me, they would have sliced your skin into deli meat. I don't know what happened to you. How could you abandon the movement and become a traitor? I am willing to overlook this if you move to Chicago. I love you, and you belong to us, not them."

Wally felt dizzy and woozy. He had to sit down and contemplate this. After twenty minutes of pondering it all, his main concern was Wendy squawking and squealing and announcing to the world what she had seen. He had zero ambitions of leaving the band and Candace for her. Sure, his interest had faded regarding the anarchist movement, and that was something he'd promised would never happen, but he also felt he was making some important strides in having the people decide how the money was spent rather than the out-of-touch politicians.

"Hi, Wendy, I will always have a special place in my heart for you, but for now, I need to continue with the band."

"Your band that protects the president? Really, Wally. You're not thinking clearly. You have been brainwashed. The wool pulled over your eyes. Please, just spend a few days with me. You will love our squat in Chicago. It will give you clarity to see what you're missing."

"I miss you too, Wendy, but what the Piss Rats is doing right now is revolutionary, and I can't ditch that."

"Wally, I didn't want it to come to this. But this isn't a choice or option. Either come to Chicago, or I tell everyone about your involvement in protecting the president, and your life is over."

Wally knew she wouldn't do this right away. He had some time. But not a lot. He would send one final communique.

"I am dating Candace, and I am committed to seeing where this and the Piss Rats go."

His phone had seizures and spasms the rest of the day, but he wouldn't let Wendy grab the steering wheel and control him. His mind was made up, and nothing could be done by her to convince him otherwise.

# VERSUS THE WORLD

O n the tour bus the next day, en route to the next show in
Connecticut, Wally said, "You know, I really thought you and
Ava would be together by now."

"Yeah, what's up with that, Mikey? You guys hang out all the
time, seem to get along great, which I find odd since you're a
punk and she's the president's assistant. But that being said, I
would never ever have guessed a month ago that Candace would
be dating Wally. What the hell do I know anymore? I do know
that life sure is outlandish. All I ever wanted was to play in a punk
band, which I am, but let's be honest. People are not interested
in the music. They're interested in watching a big-breasted stripper sing songs while having a rat on each shoulder. Then the
only other thing they care about is me pissing in the mouth of
one of those rats. We're a sideshow carnival act instead of a punk
band. Frat boys pregame in the parking lot playing beer pong
before our shows. People come dressed up as rats pretending to
get pissed on. I have seen clowns, mimes and even a guy wearing
a green man costume.

"Eddie, it's always been the Piss Rats versus the world," said Mikey. "All that ever has mattered from day one until now was saying fuck you to the world and playing our songs and doing what we want. Yes, we have now become somewhat of a novelty act, and some of the punk world considers us a sellout, but as long as we stay united, our big fucked-up family will survive the apocalypse. This is no different from the day the Piss Rats got together. We will always be facing adversity, but when we collectively say fuck you to the world, we will make it as a band until *we* decide to end it—not our fans or the media or the government or fucking aliens. I don't care if we have to play our shows in landfills, inhaling the grossest smells on earth; as long as we're playing punk rock, and being creative that's all that matters. So back to the Ava question: I found out some shit I didn't like."

"What happened?" asked Wally.

"I really don't want to talk about it right now, or ever. But you guys deserve the truth. Ava told me that she kinda encouraged Mr. Asshole to turn Johnny into a rat."

"Fucking bitch," yelled Eddie.

"Eddie, chill, man; there's more to the story. Her pops is involved with the Mob—like he is the Mob boss. She was so worried about him getting into trouble that she needed to have something she could use as blackmail. So she suggested to Mr. Asshole that he should consider Big Pharma's proposition but be very careful about going about it. This way she then had information to blackmail the government and help her dad if need be."

"Wait, how does the president's assistant kind of suggest something so monumental as this?" said Eddie.

"Well, she kind of put a gun to his head and demanded confidential material. He then told her that he was thinking about Big Pharma's proposition. So she kind of encouraged him into thinking about it more seriously."

"Kind of, kind of, kind of—what the fuck is this bullshit, Mikey?"

"So I told her I needed time to process it all and needed some space. I mean, turning our singer into a rat, father in the Mob—not sure I want to get involved in all that."

"I still blame it one hundred percent on Mr. Asshole, though. I mean, he was the one who decided while sober," said Wally.

"Fuck him, that asshole," said Eddie.

"You know, Mikey, this may sound crazy, but we really now own Ava's blackmail," said Wally.

"Huh?" said Mikey.

"Well, so Ava owned this blackmail secret…whatever. But now we basically took it from her. We made a deal with Mr. Awesome that this information would never see the light of day. So Ava's vibe was always, 'If my father gets busted, I will have Mr. Awesome release him or else I tell the public he gave Big Pharma carte blanche.' But can she really do that now? If she did, she basically screws over us or something. I don't know. What I am saying is, I think we should have a meeting with her dad and discuss it. Maybe join forces so nobody can fuck with us."

"Are you serious, Wally? A few months ago, you were this DIY hard-core punk, anti everything, no fun wussy, and now you're dating a X stripper, doing drugs with her, and suggesting we join forces with the Mob? Enough is enough. All this band ever does anymore is just dig deeper holes and get further and further away from being a punk band. I mean, do we even know how many felonies the collected bunch of us have commited?" said Eddie.

"Eddie, I agree, but listen to my rationale. We now own thirty warehouses. We hired a man who gets on all fours like a feral animal and runs around to find more people like him who we can hire. We sell out shows in hours because you're pissing into a rat's mouth. I assume people or the government are going to fuck with us. Animal right groups will be all over us soon, even though our band is vegan and we're not forcing Johnny to be pissed on. It wouldn't hurt to have some backup. Then Mikey can feel comfortable dating Ava, and we can be one big happy fucked-up family. Carla and Johnny, me and Candace, Eddie and Clash, and what about Mikey? He is going to get lonely seeing everyone on tour with a significant other besides himself. And a quick side note about the drugs you mentioned, I think were done doing those, probably done, pretty sure we are."

"Wally, that's a nice gesture, but just because we talk to Ava's dad doesn't mean we're going to be an item."

"Oh please, Mikey; you two are always together," said Wally.

"Yeah. Opposites attract, I guess," said Eddie.

# DOMINOS WILL FALL TOGETHER WE STAND BOLD AND TALL

I t was a partly cloudy spring day when the Piss Rat crew met with Ava's dad and his crew. The window was cracked in the back bar room, letting the breeze come in to mix with the deeply entrenched cigar smoke that was rooted into the furniture the way iron was found deep in the earth's molten crust.

Ava's dad had four of his men with him. Each one was dressed nicely, showcasing their talent for the finer things in life. Meanwhile, on the other side was a shoddy, tattered group of individuals minus Ava, who was dressed in all black like the rest of the Piss Rats but seemed to come off more as a professional than a punk.

She started the meeting off. "So, Dad, I am sure you're dying by now to find out why I scheduled this meeting?"

A stream of cigar smoke floated out his mouth, followed by, "I am a little curious, Ava, sure."

"You know how much I adore you and eternally wanted to be like you. When I was younger, I was always inquiring about your profession," she said in a slightly timid voice. "And you would never disclose this information to Mom or me. Well, while in college, my boyfriend and I were watching some darker films that had some Mobsters in it when he suggested that perhaps my father was in the Mob."

Her dad thought about breaking her ex-boyfriend's legs for suggesting to his daughter that he was involved in the Mob, even though he was correct. But he was too sidetracked by the sight of Candace with two rats with Mohawks perched on either shoulder to continue being angry with her ex-boyfriend. Ava continued to articulate her message, but he was too much in awe to pay attention. He couldn't stop staring at the rats.

Finally, he interrupted. "Ava, darling, I am sorry, but you're going to have to repeat everything you said. I've been mesmerized by this beautiful lady over here having two rats on her shoulder."

"Jeez, Dad, I told you all about this."

"I faintly remember, yes, but I assumed it was an analogy. You know, 'I am so stressed from the rat race that it feels like there is a rat on each shoulder.' I didn't actually think it was bona fide legit."

"Yes, it's all very authentic and the reason we are here, Dad. When I eventually found out you were in the Mob and realized that you would sooner or later get busted or worse, I decided to spend the rest of my life making sure I could blackmail somebody in case you got into trouble. Didn't you ever wonder how I all of a sudden became the president's assistant?"

"I just figured you had your father's work ethic. If you want to play hard, well, you better work hard. Nothing is free."

"I do. You instilled in me a feverish value system that taught me if you want to be successful in life, you must break a sweat. But sometimes, no matter how hard you work, how smart you are, there can be obstacles that need attention. When I finally resigned myself to the fact that there was no quick way to obtain blackmail-worthy information, an opportunity presented itself, and I had minutes to decide. I saw the president's assistant at the museum, and when she went into the bathroom, that's when I pulled my gun on her and suggested it would be wise if she resigned and I took her place."

Ava's dad and his crew's faces were affected by this revelation, changing from expressions of dull interest to aroused enthrallment.

"So when I became the president's assistant, I then put another gun to the president's head and asked him if he had any top-secret information he could tell me."

One of Ava's dad's crew members spoke up. "Boss, maybe we should hire her. Two stickups with no help or experience is impressive."

A different one spoke up. "Like father, like daughter; must be in the genes."

Her father smiled slightly, showing his gold tooth, and then urged Ava to continue.

"Anyway, I finally uncovered some info that I could use to blackmail the president and help you when this band, the Piss Rats"— she pointed to them—"accidentally stole it."

This apparently was the signal to Ava's dad's crew to stand up and flex their muscles. A flustered Ava said, "Calm down. It was by accident, and I kind of like their bassist and am going to be their tour manager and oversee all thirty warehouses. We believe owning the warehouses and touring nonstop with Eddie pissing into Johnny's mouth, along with collecting others who have special features, will create problems. That's where you come in, Daddy," said Ava in an attempt to act youthful to influence her father. For Daddy had a tough time denying a cute Ava anything. "So what we're thinking is, perhaps we could all help one another out and make this all work."

Her pensive dad nodded, and with a brush of the hand, he suggested they all leave while he talked with his crew. They all went outside and were feeling a bit flustered about what they were doing. Sure, Ava had had some experience with this stuff, since this was her father and she'd already pulled a gun twice, but this was new territory for the Piss Rats.

"I know this all sounds crazy, joining up with my dad, but he's really smart and talented, and I know you guys in retrospect will see this as a good decision."

Candace thought about her days as a stripper and told herself, *This ain't nothing. I saw a lot worse. Drunken adults who think they can toss me around like some pretty little doll not knowing that I am pretty good at kickboxing and in a sadistic way, enjoy watching them suffer endless punches and kicks to their faces.*

Mikey told himself he could handle this since he was the one who came up with the pinball idea and had enough courage built up from that to handle Mob stuff.

Wally told himself that if he could date a X stripper, then he could handle working with the Mob.

Eddie thought about how there should be a Facebook where you post just the negative stuff…instead of the current site, which was primarily positive. He then worked on a new joke. "What's up with all these guys wearing spandex like chicks do while they go jogging? The problem is, from behind I think there a chick, and then they're not. I mean, come on; just put on a pair of shorts so I don't have to guess which gender of an ass I am seeing."

One of Ava's men instructed them to come back in. They all sat down again.

"So we have all talked, and we have agreed to your proposition. We think both parties can benefit from working together. Chuck will oversee this project."

Chuck stood up and introduced himself to everybody and briefly explained their initial plans. "You will now be traveling with a personal bodyguard. You will pay him like he is a member of your band. Then each of your warehouses will have a security team. This might be too much or too little. See what happens, and play it by ear."

As they were leaving, Wally snuck back inside, claiming he'd left his wallet on the couch.

"Hey, guys, since we're now working together, I already have a situation in Chicago that needs attention. But no violence. Simply show up and let them know we're serious."

"This is what we were born to do, Wally. You can sleep soundly knowing this will be taken care of, minus the violence. However, if they choose to ignore our complementary nice warning, then there will be some black and blue painted on their pretty little canvases."

"I understand, but please no violence, no matter how they respond. And I look forward to working with you."

They nodded and said, "Take care."

Wally strolled out of the building, feeling for the first time like a little part of him was unbreakable and that those around him who'd thought they could walk all over him were wrong.

# NEVER A DULL MOMENT

At the next show in Baltimore, Charlie was out and about doing his thing when he noticed a woman shuffling around in her purse with what appeared to be many fingers. He clandestinely trailed her, hoping for another glance before approaching her. After thirty minutes of following her with no success, he knew he would have to be more direct. So he bumped into her, and as she withdrew her hands from her jacket pocket, he finally had the proof he needed to initiate a conversation.

"I am so sorry to bother you, miss, but can I buy you a cup of coffee?"

"It's no problem, and I think I will pass on the offer, but thanks."

"Listen, I saw your hands. You don't have to live in secrecy and embarrassment—there is another way. If I can just talk to you for a few minutes."

The few minutes turned into two hours, and Grace told Charlie she was very interested in what he had to offer her.

While in Virginia, Charlie hit up the James River Park to see if he could find anybody. While strolling through the beautiful foliage, he saw out of the corner of his eye a man whose tongue stretched out at least five feet in the air. The man was able to extend his tongue and satisfy an itch on his ankle. Then his tongue darted outward and came in contact with a tree branch, where it hovered for two minutes before returning back to his mouth.

In North Carolina, Charlie rented a bike and began riding down the streets when he spotted a man climbing up a tree in less than a minute and then jumping onto another tree. The man then jumped down off the tree and proceeded to hop from car to car.

Charlie was up to fifty people he had rescued. Most of them worked in the pinball warehouses.

Grace had joined the Pinball Punks, playing the banjo. Having ten extra fingers, she made sounds come out of the banjo that had never been heard before.

Lucy was touring with the Piss Rats as security, along with one of Ana's dad's men. With shows now exceeding ten thousand people, the Piss Rats were depending on Lucy's eyes to determine when there was trouble brewing. She stood on the corner of the stage, and on the opposite end of the stage was one of Ava's men. His job was to use binoculars and watch Lucy's eyes. When they turned black, he knew there was going to be an issue.

It was February, and the Piss Rats were on their third month of touring. Their next stop was Portland. They wanted to tour with all their favorite bands, so the lineups were constantly rotating. The Northwest tour lineup was: The Goddman Gallows, Everymen, Filthy Still, Days N Daze, Long Knife, Implaers and Glue.

Eddie would call up each band to persuade them that they were still a DIY punk band and not a sideshow act. He pointed out that by touring with the Piss Rats they would first and foremost have their music reach people it normally would not and isn't that every musician's goal? With each show being sold out, the energy was unparalleled he explained. Also, it was a good pay day.

But the truth was tough to disguise and hide. It was clear they resembled more of a sideshow than a punk band. They had gone from four members to eight now. Their entire crew was twenty people. During "Pinball Punks, Politicians Stink Like Skunks," the band had everybody on stage.

Jed was now eight feet tall.

Charlie was running back and forth on all fours.

Grace was busy making the banjo do things it had never done before.

Lucy quickly adopted the punk rock look, dressed in mostly black, tattoos, piercings, and Chuck Taylors.

Dan was on the corner of the stage with his long tongue. In the middle of the set, a massive number of flies were released in the air, and Dan's impressive tongue was able to sweep them all up, amazing the crowd and taking them further into the circus sideshow theme.

Ava's dad's man, Mark, was watching Lucy's eyes when they suddenly turned black. He got goose bumps on his arm. He raced out of his seat to see what was causing her eyes to turn the shade of night. He couldn't believe what he saw. There were a dozen monkeys on stage. They took to Jed's long frame the most. He had three monkeys on him as he wiggled and thrust, trying to remove them. Everybody was worried sick about Carla and Johnny. The monkeys would definitely try to attack them. Candace reached up and grabbed one of the rats, but when she went to grab the other rat, it was missing. Candace felt a pain so deep she almost collapsed. Then out of nowhere, there was a monkey running through the crowd with a rat on its neck. The Piss Rats concluded that Johnny was handling the monkey problem just fine and started playing again. It was pure chaos. Johnny Piss Rat was still riding the monkey as it went ballistic trying to remove him. The monkey was jumping on and off the rails and on the food stands, and running through the crowd.

Eight-foot-tall Jed still had monkeys crawling on him like he was a small tree.

Grace was playing her banjo while the monkeys tried eating her fingers, thinking they were baby bananas.

The next morning, the Piss Rats and their crew met up with Ava's dad and their crew.

"So I called this emergency meeting because of last night. Obviously, we're all worried about this happening again in the future. With Johnny and Carla being the entire reason the Piss Rats are drawing such huge crowds and also being such small, easy targets, we need to rethink security."

Ava's dad's train of thought was interrupted by Jed, who had gone into full-out freak mode, still trying to rid his body of anything healthy. He had long blue dreadlocks and was holding a gallon of rum while smoking a huge joint. Every few minutes, he was also spraying vinegar into his mouth, resulting in a twisted, gnarly facial expression.

"Our initial theory after talking with some people is that the monkeys were released by the government. They hoped the monkeys would wipe out Johnny and Carla. Since they failed, we can expect them to continue this until they're successful. We're going to assign three more security guards to your crew. That will be four total. You will have to compensate for this. However, we will give you the highest possible discount, since we are working together and I want my daughter safe."

# DEAD TREES DYED GREEN

Every so often, the Piss Rats would see a man in the crowd with a moustache meandering off. This man knew his cover was blown, causing a tingling, buzzing, thrilling feeling inside him. He was not forgiven and never would be. Nobody told him to leave. But there was a new awareness of his circumstances and actions. In a befouled sense, they understand how Mr. Awesome could succumb to the twenty million, but they were also disgusted with him because they'd agreed to the one hundred thousand dollars each not knowing anything repugnant would develop, while Mr. Awesome knew a nefarious pot of poison was brewing with his twenty million. The Piss Rats realized just how carcinogenic money could be. They could have passed up this tour. Remained relatively content with their prior existence. But when faced with such large sums of money, they naively believed in their hearts it would go smoothly.

So they knew that when $20 million was offered to Mr. Awesome, it was like dancing with the devil, and most would dance it. In the end, like Wally always said, "Will you make the world better or worse with your actions? What will your footprint and contribution to society be?" The Piss Rats were steadfast in using the money to make the world a better place. They would never stop seeking out and helping those who were the victims of greedy bastards and feverishly work on keeping their ethics right in front them.

## The End

# EPILOGUE

"Oh my God, Eddie, that was amazing. How did you last an hour?"

"Shit, I could have gone another hour or four hours. The first night on the tour bus, we all partied relentlessly with unwavering dedication and passed out hard-core. So Mr. Awesome had a doctor clandestinely inject our hands with a highly potent but safe metal so we could play pinball for hours without our hands getting tired. In retrospect, it was really so the pharmaceuticals wouldn't leach into our hands while playing pinball. After he explained how people in all industries use it, including porn, I thought about it from time to time. After we told him about the audio of him confessing, I sent him a text message later that night to see if he could have my cock injected with it. He said, 'Sure. Why not at this point?' So this is permanent, babe."

Eddie thought about organizing an orgy with Ava, and Candace. The goal would be to impress them to the point that the president's assistant and the X stripper would leave and the Piss Rats could start resembling a punk band again.

He looks over to Clash with that beaming electric vibe pulsating throughout her body and he thinks maybe everything doesn't need to be put under a punk microscope. His girl was happy, he has plenty of money, tons of people saw his band nightly and Johnny is found.

"I love you Clash."

Clash is now in heaven with Joe Strummer.

# ABOUT THE AUTHOR

Dave Anderson's obsession with punk began twenty-five years ago. He plays bass but, unlike the Piss Rats, never managed to get a band together.

An avid biker and outdoor enthusiast, Anderson lives in Philadelphia with his wife, Ashley, and their two cats, Iggy and Mike. When he's not biking, he's honing his black-and-white photography skills, drinking different types of beer, and adding to his extensive vinyl collection. He owns more hats than any one person needs, reads a few books a week, and designs his own Chuck Taylors.

www.ingramcontent.com/pod-product-compliance
Lightning Source LLC
Chambersburg PA
CBHW061200170626
46809CB00003B/1187